MW01087504

Praise for Jenn.
USA TODAY calls *Crave* a must-read romance

"*Crave* gets the balance between lust filled scenes and a meaningful plot just right. Neither takes from the other and together they just add up to a very satisfying and emotional read." —Between My Lines

"If you love Foster, Kaye and Dawson's *Something New* series you'll love *Crave* and the Undone series." —Caffeinated Book Reviewer.

"Every character in this book (*Sinful*) is amazingly written. " — Bookish Bevil

"You know why I love this author? She takes something absolutely mundane like a "Best Friend's Sister" romance and turns it into a masterpiece." —For the Love of Fictional Worlds

"*Crave* by Jennifer Dawson is a darkly erotic and deeply moving romance."-—Romance Novel News

"Jennifer Dawson's *Sinful* has amazing scenes that get my heart beating and calls for a cold shower, but the love story that is evolving between Leo and Jillian is amazing."—Courting Fiction

Other books by Jennifer Dawson

Something New Series

Take A Chance on Me
The Winner Takes It All
The Name of the Game
As Good as New (Coming March 2016)

Undone Series

Crave
Sinful
Unraveled
Debauched (Coming April, 2016)

UNRAVELED

Jennifer Dawson

This is a work of fiction. Names, characters, places, and incidents either are the product of the author's imagination or are used fictitiously, and any resemblance to actual persons, living or dead, business establishments, events or locales is entirely coincidental.

The author has asserted their rights under the Copyright Designs and Patent Acts 1988 (as amended) to be identified as the author of this book.

1.

Jillian

"Please tell me this isn't happening, Jillian." My brother, Michael's voice is pained. His forehead creased.

Expression somber, I nod. "It's happening."

"This is not how I want to spend Valentine's Day," he says, a scowl marring his handsome face.

Helplessly, I shrug. "Neither do I, but what can we do? It's out of our hands."

He stands there in the doorway leading to the condo he shares with his girlfriend, Layla. "Are we really going to do this?"

"We are," I say in my most grave tone. "Let's not think of our mother."

His face twists and he winces. "Don't bring her into this."

I understand. It's hard. The biggest trauma in our sibling relationship. I lower my eyes. "Dad would be so disappointed."

Next to me my fiancé, Leo, who also happens to be Michael's best friend, pinches me. "Be nice, can't you see he's suffering?"

I do see. But I'm Michael's little sister; this is much harder on him than it is on me. I fight the grin twitching at my lips.

Michael's hand tightens on the doorknob. "If you're concerned about our father, you could stay home."

"I would." I shake my head and cast a sideways glance at Leo. "But he won't let me."

Leo shoots me an exasperated eye roll.

Unashamed, I continue, really twisting the knife into my brother's heart. "He's unreasonable. He won't take no for an answer." I let my eyes grow wide while I lower my voice. "He spanks me, like, all the time."

Michael grimaces, but the faintest of smiles flickers. "Knowing you, I'm sure you had it coming."

Leo shakes his head. "Believe me she did."

I tap the heel of one knee-high leather boot. "Some brother you are. We're family."

This is the unfortunate consequence of having a dominant fiancé and brother when all your kinks are right there in the open. They tend to side against me.

Michael raises a brow. "Back to the point, it's not too late to go home. Save us all the family humiliation."

"Sorry, not going to happen." I flutter my lashes. "We'll just have to learn to live with it."

Leo sighs, and when he speaks his tone is amused. "You'll both survive."

Michael narrows his gaze on Leo. "Easy for you to say, I don't see your sisters here."

Leo's hand slides territorially around my hip and gives me his sly glance. "Lucky for me, my sisters aren't like that."

Surprised laughter spurts from my lips and I elbow the love of my life in the ribs. "Hey! What's wrong with *that*?"

Leo kisses the top of my head. "Not a thing, I mean, it's fine for *his* sister, but *my* sisters are too pure for that."

He's teasing, of course. Just one of the many perks he gets from being engaged to his best friend's baby sister.

I have to play my part accordingly. I jerk away and plant my hands on my red latex-covered hips. "I didn't hear any complaints this morning."

I'm pretty sure most of the stuff Leo did to me is illegal in most states, but believe me, I'm not complaining. Leo's a sexual genius.

What can I say? I'm a lucky girl.

"Stop. Not another word." Michael growls. Apparently he's in overprotective big brother mode, and looks quite menacing standing there in all black, with that set of his granite-like jaw and high cheekbones. "I don't want to hear this, nor do I want to do this."

I roll my eyes at my brother. "We've all had to make sacrifices."

It's our friend, Brandon Townsend III's, big night. This weekend he's opening his brand new club—a modern-day speakeasy—that's literally the talk of the Chicago club scene. Unlike his current place, this isn't a sex club, and the waiting list is a mile long. Tonight is a special occasion, a Valentine's treat. Brandon is holding a very exclusive VIP party for all his kinky friends. According to him, he can't go too straight; he's got a rep to live up to.

My brother doesn't appreciate there are people that would kill for a chance to go to one of Brandon's parties that he takes for granted. I don't make that mistake. I have connections to make. I'm going to be an art dealer once I finish my masters. I mean, sure, making contacts at a sex party isn't ideal, but you never know when the CEO of a company, that likes to be trussed up and hogtied, is going to need some art for his corner office.

"Just shoot me," Michael says in a droll voice.

"That can be arranged, I have a gun," Leo quips, good-natured. Leo and Michael are homicide detectives at the Chicago Police Department. Bloodshed is a regular topic in these circles.

There's a female exasperated huff from behind Michael's broad, six-five shoulders. "Are you going to let them in or just stand there blocking their way?"

Michael's jaw turns hard and he glances back at Layla, whom I still can't see. "Are you getting sassy with me, girl?"

A laugh. "They've been standing in the hallway for five minutes while you complain. At least let them sit on the couch."

"Yeah! Let me in," I say in my best annoying little sister voice.

Leo grips my elbow. "I suppose we should take pity on him."

"Well, I would if he would let me in the door." I huff again for good measure.

Leo winks at me, and then grins at Michael. "It would be nice if you let us in."

Before he can respond, Layla ducks under his arm still blocking the threshold and straightens to her full five-seven.

One look at her and I let out a low wolf whistle. She's gorgeous with wild chestnut hair she's curled into something exotic and untamed. Her sky-blue eyes are smoky and heavily made up. Her dress is white, short, and silky. In more polite circles her outfit might be considered more appropriate as a nightgown, but on her it looks exactly right. She's clearly not wearing a bra and her white boots go up to her knees.

She looks insane, like a go-go sex goddess, with no trace of the haunted girl I'd met nine months ago.

"Jillian's here." She throws her arms around me in a hug.

I squeeze her and then pull back to look at her. "Goddamn, girl. You're smoking."

She beams. "Why thank you, so are you."

She's right, I am. I'm wearing a red latex fetish dress with a short flirty skirt that plays up my Amazon height, endless legs and makes my waist impossibly small in a corseted top. Leo laced me into the dress and would be lacing me out of it sometime tonight. I didn't know when, but it was a matter of time, and the anticipation was already killing me.

What can I say, I like to be watched.

A kink I had no idea about until I started going out with Leo, who likes to push me to my limits. We've been together for almost a year now and he's pulled me farther and farther into my submissive side, much to my brother's dismay.

Which brought us to tonight where our worlds are colliding.

Not that we all didn't know about each other's proclivities. Layla and I were known to get into trouble together quite often.

You've got to keep these men on their toes.

Leo pulls Layla close, running his hands affectionately and mildly inappropriately over her stomach. He kisses the side of her neck and grins at Michael. "I can't wait to see what you do to all this bare skin tonight."

I've learned over time that the BDSM crowd tends to be a bit more handsy than most would consider polite.

I've gotten used to it.

My brother gave him a dry look. "I can't say I feel the same."

While Layla and I have been "dealt with" a time or two (or many) in front of each other, Michael and Leo keep it pretty tame. But tame and Valentine's sex parties don't really go hand and hand, and my brother is having a hard time adjusting. Not that I can't relate, when Michael puts Layla through whatever he's got planned I won't be anywhere in the vicinity.

But I can still have fun with it in the spaces in-between.

Because I'm still a little sister, and giving my big brother fits is kind of like a job requirement.

Layla grabs my hand and we duck under my brother's arm and walk into their condo. Their dog Belle leaps from the couch and runs over to me in excited circles. My brother rescued her from the streets a couple years ago. She's so mangy and pitiful looking she's completely adorable. She's also the worst trained dog ever.

When she tries to plant her huge paws on my stomach, Layla barks, "Belle, down."

The dog promptly sits, and looks at Layla with panting, excited eyes.

I'm in shock. Before Layla, Belle was a lovable, overly

affectionate wild beast that wouldn't listen to anyone, least of all Michael. "Wow! I'm impressed."

Layla strokes the dog's ears. "Good girl."

Belle stares at her in worship and doesn't move from her spot.

I pat her on her head and her whole body shakes as her tail pounds against the hardwood floor, but she still stays seated.

I whip toward my big, scary brother. "Layla's trained her. She listens."

He narrows his eyes. "Don't remind me."

Layla leans down, flashing all sorts of cleavage, and pats Belle on the head, who whines with excitement. "That's right, girl. He's too easy on you." She tosses a mischievous glance at Michael. "Later I'll teach you how to give a proper command."

I cover my mouth to keep from laughing, but Leo has no problem and the sound of his rich voice rings through the living room.

Michael crosses his arms over his chest and shakes his head. "You just can't help yourself, can you?"

"Nope." Her voice is flippant. The more time that passes the sassier Layla becomes and I have to say it's pretty awesome.

My brother practically pulled her back from the dead, and she's been thriving ever since. When I first met her, it worried me to watch Michael so enraptured with someone so broken, but I see now he wasn't wrong to love her. She's the best thing that ever happened to him, because he needs someone that's a constant challenge.

And Layla is a challenge.

With a sweet, innocent expression, Layla points to the floor. "Down, Belle."

The dog promptly falls to the floor and plants her head on paws, looking pitifully adorable. Layla flashes Michael a grin. "It's all in the tone."

He cocks a brow. "Is it now?"

Layla flips her hair. "I'm surprised you don't know that."

I recognize her look, the amused defiance, I've used it on

Leo many times and he indulges me when he feels like it.

The question is if Michael is in the mood to indulge Layla.

Michael slants a glance at Leo. "She's giving me no choice here, is she?"

Leo shakes his head. "No, she is not."

Michael assesses Layla then points to the floor. "You can come to heel right next to Belle, girl."

So he's not in the mood.

Something flashes in Layla's blue eyes. "I don't want to."

Michael shrugs. "Too bad. Kneel."

I flash her a look of sympathy, although it's really her own fault. I didn't know my brother was a dominant—or even what a dominant was—until I started dating Leo. But now that our dirty secrets are all out in the open, both Michael and Leo are more overt in their displays as long as we're not with the rest of the family.

Although we've never done anything like we're going to do tonight. We did grumble. One night when Leo and I were over at Brandon's for dinner I protested it as inhumane, but Brandon ordered us all to get over ourselves, exclaiming he'd never speak to us again if we didn't show up.

I accused Brandon of being a dramatic schoolgirl.

Which ended up with me turned over Leo's knee while Brandon watched in amusement.

Sure it was embarrassing, but I still came.

Layla stands there, not obeying. She glances at me, but I can only shrug helplessly.

"Layla," Michael says, his tone full of warning. "I'm not going to tell you again. Trust me, you won't like the consequences."

Layla gives an indignant little sigh and sinks to her knees.

Michael walks over to her, strokes her hair and whispers something in her ear that makes her gasp.

Leo's arm comes around my waist and he kisses my temple. "Look at you, being such a good girl."

My heart swells ridiculously, because I like to make him proud. I bat my lashes up at him. "Always."

7

Leo's head dips and his lips brush my ear. "Later, I'm going to put you on display. Everyone is going to watch you and they're all going to see exactly what kind of girl you are."

My knees actually go weak.

He's been working me over all day and I'm about to combust. He's brought me close to orgasm about a hundred times, but I haven't come.

And, I want to come.

You have no idea how bad I want to come.

"I can't wait to sink my cock into that hot, tight cunt of yours." Leo's teeth scrapes my earlobe. "In front of everyone."

My whole body goes tight with fear, anticipation and arousal. I take a stuttery breath and look up at him. "You wouldn't."

His eyes darken. "I would. I am."

I swallow hard.

"I'm going to lay you out, expose you, and fuck you."

"Oh god."

He smirks. "Indeed. Consider it a Valentine's present."

I bite my lip and twist the antique, platinum diamond engagement ring on my finger. He's giving me my fantasy and it makes me nervous as well as excited. He's dug deep into my exhibitionist side, testing and seeking out the things that flip my switch. The only person I've ever done anything in front of before is Brandon because he's a friend and he's safe. But as my boundaries have stretched, so have my limits, and my fantasies have become increasingly depraved. I thought that was where they would stay. Leo's never done anything like this. Never fucked me in front of anyone. Never exposed me for just anyone to see.

I'm terrified.

Even as the fear rushes through me, wetness slicks down my bare thighs, because, of course, I'm not wearing any panties.

I'd had some on, but Leo shredded them off me with a knife, then licked my pussy until I twisted under him, pulling back when I was about to come.

I grip the counter.

Leo's mouth brushes my neck, his tongue sliding over my skin. "That's right. Everyone's going to be watching you. Are you wet, Jilly?"

"Yes."

"Do you want everyone to watch you?"

I'm not thinking about the sanity of my answers. "Yes."

"Are you going to please me?"

"Yes." He makes me a mindless needy mess and all I want at the moment is to continue.

But before he can, the doorbell rings.

He strokes a finger down my bare arm. "I believe you will."

2.

Ruby

I don't know what I'm doing here. I almost turned around and went home about a hundred times on the Uber ride over. The only thing that stopped me was Layla. She invited me to this party and I don't want to disappoint her.

It's not like I'm a prude or anything, but sex parties aren't really my thing. I agreed because I was curious, and have second-guessed my decision ever since.

Michael, my best friend Layla's boyfriend, lets me in. He smiles and wraps me up in a big bear hug that makes me feel like a miniature person. I'm only five-three, practically tiny next to Michael's tallness. "Ruby, glad you decided to come along. Come on in."

"Thanks for the invite," I say in my most breezy voice. I'm beyond nervous to be doing something so outside my comfort zone, but I don't want anyone to notice.

I walk into Michael and Layla's living room to find Layla kneeling on the floor, wearing an obscene white dress that hardly leaves anything to the imagination. Unable to hide my shock, I let out a surprised, "Oh."

Layla flashes me a sly little grin before giving Michael a dark look.

Michael laughs. "Layla's working on a bit of an attitude adjustment right now, what can I get you to drink?"

I bite my bottom lip as a stab of jealousy twists in my chest. A jealousy I don't understand or want, but seems to grow every time I see Layla and Michael. Even engaged in their kinky behavior, they are just so together. So very in love. It's a stark reminder that Layla has managed to share this bond with two men—her fiancé that passed away and Michael—while I haven't managed to find it once.

I clear my throat and try to pretend it's perfectly normal that she's kneeling on the floor, patting her dog, Belle, and scowling at the love of her life. "I'll take whatever you have. I'm not picky."

I turn to Leo and Jillian, who've I've gotten to know quite well over the last nine months. They're also in the so-called "lifestyle" and look positively gorgeous together with their dark hair and olive skin. Like Michael, Leo's wearing all black, and Jillian is decked out in some sort of red dress I can't even figure out how she got on. The top is a tight corset she looks sewn into and the skirt is a flirty little fabric that barely reaches mid-thigh on her ridiculously long legs. She's tall—at least five nine or ten—and looks like an Amazon warrior princess.

Leo strokes his hand down her rubber-encased hip and Jillian gives me a glassy-eyed, slightly unfocused smile before waving hello.

Leo winks at me. "You're looking lovely tonight, Ruby."

"Thanks," I say, the response automatic, although I'm not sure it's true. I'm pretty enough, but in my short, black skirt, studded belt, and black tank top I'm dressed all wrong.

Layla and Jillian look like sex and sin. Every man that sees them tonight will want them. Lust after them and covet what Michael and Leo have. I, on the other hand, look like a pixie rock princess. Like I'm dressed for a Halloween party instead of to be ravished on Valentine's Day.

And what was I thinking going out with the two most in-love couples on earth the night of single girl hell? I should be out with Ashley and my other hangout girlfriends, trolling the dance scene as we all try and forget that we're not attached.

What can I say? Curiosity got the best of me, as it always does. Curiosity my conservative, Christian parents have warned me about since I could walk. As a child, growing up in a small town in Indiana, their number-one mantra was—*be careful, Ruby*. Of course, I rebelled, and pretty much got into any trouble I could find. Which, I suppose, is why I agreed to come tonight.

A decision I'm pretty sure is a mistake. I've been here one minute and I already feel out of place, like a fifth wheel. It's not that I don't love hanging out with my best friend, because I do. I love Michael and all that he's done to help Layla heal from the murder of her fiancé. And Leo and Jillian are fun to be around and a guaranteed good time. I know they'll do everything in their power to make sure I'm included.

It's just that usually we're at a bar or restaurant and everything is totally normal. Like being with regular couples. But tonight, going to some sort of fetish party to kick off the opening of their friend Brandon's club, I'm out of my element.

I know I should consider myself lucky, when my friend Ashley heard I'd scored an invite to the hottest ticket in town, she'd begged me to let her come, but it's not my kind of scene. If we were going to a metal club, I'd be totally fine, but I'm not into BDSM, nor do I want to be. I'm tagging along for the experience, to say I've seen it firsthand. To prove to myself I'm not the closet conservative I sometimes fear I am.

But after five minutes I realize my mistake. Leo and Michael are in full domination mode, and I can't avoid it. Sometimes when we go out, I sense the undercurrent of what Layla calls the power dynamic between them. Occasionally, Michael will take her by the neck and say something in her ear with a certain look on his face that will make Layla shudder, but for the most part, they act pretty normal. Tonight all bets are off, I'll be unable to escape what they are. The air practically pulses with it. Proof positive by the fact that I've walked in to Layla kneeling on the floor, saying nothing.

Not that I want to be dominated, because *I do not*. I've asked Layla enough questions to understand the basics and it's not for me. I can't stand the thought of someone trying to control me. But I can't deny I find I'm fascinated despite myself. In moments of introspection, I've determined it's the dedication and focus dominant men seem to possess that intrigues me.

I've never had a man pay attention to me the way Michael and Leo pay attention to their women. Unlike Layla, who clearly has a knack for picking perfect men, I have the exact opposite problem.

I have terrible taste in men.

I can't even deny it.

I'm always attracted to the wrong sort. Emotional, temperamental rocker boys are like crack to me. I mean, I'm hardly the first girl to be attracted to musicians. Intensely creative types that lose themselves in their poetry and guitars.

I'm also that type. I'm a graphic artist by day, and singer by night.

They are my people.

Unfortunately, men like that tend to have Peter Pan complexes.

Which, I actually don't mind. Even at the ripe old age of thirty, I'm not in a hurry to be a grown up. Sure, I have a job, my own apartment, and I pay my bills, but that's as far as it goes. As far as I want it to go. I have no interest in a conventional, traditional life. I don't want a husband, kids and a mortgage.

I grew up like that—in Pleasantville—with parents that love each other. My mom and dad have a good, solid traditional marriage and they raised my brother and sister and me to have family values. My siblings toe the party line; walk the straight and narrow, living within a five-mile radius of my parents' house, in the small Indiana town where I grew up. They raise their kids, go to church on Sunday, PTA meetings, and potluck dinners at the neighbors. Don't get me wrong, there's nothing wrong with that life at all. It's the American dream.

It's just not my dream.

I don't want to be ordinary.

I want to live my life on the fringe. I want to stay up all night drinking bad coffee and talking about philosophy. I want to roll out of bed at eleven. Follow my impulses. Live without schedules and restrictions. So the fact that I attract men that aren't interested in grown-up life is nobody's fault but my own.

Michael hands me a martini glass, pulling me from my rambling thoughts. "Layla made lemon drops for you girls."

"Thanks, Laylay," I say, calling her by her college nickname. We were paired up as roommates our freshmen year, and despite our differences, we have been best friends ever since. She's the best friend I could ever ask for. She understands me and I understand her. We'd walk through fire for each other. Unfortunately for her, she was forced to travel a dark road, and I stayed by her side the whole time, even when she infuriated me.

Layla glances at Michael and he nods. She shifts her attention to me and says, "You're welcome."

I grin down at her. "What'd you do?"

She pouts, her thick, heavily mascaraed eyes batting at Michael. "Absolutely nothing."

"I'm totally unreasonable, aren't I?" Michael strokes her hair affectionately.

"Totally," Layla says.

And I experience a stab of envy at the love on Michael's face as he looks down at her.

Jillian pours a glass for herself. "Layla makes the best drinks."

The doorbell rings and I frown. "Who's that?"

Michael goes to the door and Leo says, "Chad."

Oh no. Layla conveniently forgot to tell me she invited, Chad Fellows. I'd suspect a set up except it's pretty clear we're not each other's type, despite the fact that over the past couple months he has become my unofficial date when neither of us has one.

From what Layla told me, she went out on a blind date with Chad, thrust upon her by her sister right around the time she met Michael. Apparently, three or four months ago, Michael and Layla ran into Chad on a date and they all hit it off. They'd started hanging out, going on double dates with the other couple, until Chad broke up with the girl he'd been seeing. She'd disappeared, but he'd stuck, becoming part of the group.

I have nothing against Chad. I actually like him a lot. He's a perfectly nice, solid guy. He's just a bit traditional for my tastes. Yes, he's good looking in an All American, Abercrombie and Fitch way. All tall, lean muscles and broad shoulders, with that killer jaw, high cheekbones and nice crystal-clear, blue eyes. He's also got short, expertly messy brown hair, and a good mouth.

He's the kind of guy you bring home to your parents. The settling-down type. As an IT manager, with a good nine-to-five job, he's actually kind of a catch.

If you like that kind of thing.

If I brought a guy like Chad home to my mother, she'd be on her knees thanking Jesus that her daughter had finally seen reason.

Michael opens the door and the man in question walks in. In gray pants, a white button-down, and messy bedroom hair, he looks good. He wasn't the least bit nerdy or anything, he just didn't look dark and dangerous like Leo and Michael. He looks harmless. Clean cut.

What was he even doing coming to a fetish party? He belonged even less than I did. Those dominant girls were going to eat him for breakfast if he wasn't careful.

At least watching him fumble around would keep me entertained.

As he strolls in he doesn't even seem to pause at Layla kneeling on the floor. He glances down at her, but there's no flicker of surprise like I would have expected. He hands Michael a bottle of wine, shakes Leo's hand, and gives Jillian a kiss on the cheek before waving at me. "Hey, Ruby."

I wave back. "Hey, Chad."

He winks at me. "Glad you came along to keep me company."

"Me too." I relax a bit. He might not be my type, but at least I won't be an odd man out. And we get along so well it's hard to be put out.

He gives Jillian a long, appraising nod before flashing a grin at Leo. "Well done."

Leo laughs. "I agree."

Michael places the bottle on the counter, and says, "Be right back."

When he walks out of the room and down the hallway Leo says to Chad, "Wait until you see what I do to her later."

Jillian flushes, gasps, and glares at her boyfriend. "Don't say that."

I blink. That was overt. Leo will give poor Chad a heart attack before he even gets to the party.

What am I doing here again? I could be at The Whisky, watching one of my favorite bands. I have my eye on the bass player, although so did a lot of females, so I've been playing hard to get.

I wasn't sure it was working though.

Chad's brow rises, and he looks at Jillian like she's a horse up for auction. "I hope I get a front row seat."

Leo turns his attention on Jillian, his gaze raking over her. "I think that can be arranged."

"Leo," Jillian hisses. "Stop that."

Leo kisses her soundly on the lips before twisting his hand in her hair, and saying to Chad, "Being watched makes her wet."

At his words shock rolls through me. I want to look away but find I can't. I expect Chad to be shocked too, but instead he leans in and whispers something in Jillian's ear that has her swallowing hard.

Where's his surprise?

My whole body flushes hot and I finally tear my gaze away.

Michael walks back in and Leo releases his hold on Jillian.

Chad turns to me, an easy smile on his face. "No Valentine's date tonight, Ruby?"

I can only stare at him, confused and vaguely out of sorts. Why isn't he taken aback, like I am? How is he able to adapt the easy manner I've been shooting for since I walked in?

"Nope," I say lamely. A bad feeling vibrates in my chest and suddenly I want to go home. This is too much information. Too much... something. "Where's your date?"

I suppose this isn't really the kind of place you bring just anyone.

He shrugs. "Casual dates don't really go over too well on Valentine's day." He gives me his winning, got-to-love-me smile. "Too many expectations."

I laugh and the tension in my shoulders eases a bit. "Exactly."

He grabs the beer Michael offers and winks at Layla. "Got yourself in trouble there, did ya?"

Layla sticks out her tongue at him.

Chad rubs his jaw, lightly dusted with stubble, and says to Michael, "I don't think she's sorry."

Michael flicks a glance down at her. "Are you sorry, girl?"

"Of course," Layla says, her voice saccharine sweet.

"And what are you sorry for?" Michael walks and stands in front of her. At six-five he towers over her on the floor and she looks small and delicate.

She meets his gaze and licks her lips. "I'm very sorry Belle only listens to me."

He crouches down, takes her by the throat and she gasps. "I see you're in the mood to be bratty tonight."

"Me? Never?" The words a husky, gasping sound.

I hold my breath.

This is much more explicit than I'm used to them being.

He gives her a smile that would have me shaking in my boots, but all it does is flush Layla's cheeks a pretty pink. "You're in the mood to be bratty. I'm in the mood to be unreasonable. This should be an interesting evening, don't you think?"

"Yes," she says, her tone all breathless and clearly wanting.

He straightens, crossing his arms as he looks down at her. "Since I'm stuck in this hell with my sister, let's take care of that attitude in the bedroom."

Without a word she rises to her feet.

Her dress is short, silky and leaves almost nothing to the imagination. She is a beautiful girl, but tonight she looks otherworldly gorgeous. And sexy in a way I can't even fathom. I don't understand how Michael can be so possessive over her, so utterly devoted, and still be fine letting her walk around like that.

Michael twines his fingers through her hair. "A few strikes with the cane should set you right, don't you think?"

Out of the corner of my eye I see Jillian wince, and I assume this is not a pleasant experience. I mean, how could it be? A cane? I flush hot.

Layla, always a brave girl, says, "I didn't really do anything wrong."

Michael raises a brow. "You're not being sassy and a bit bratty?"

"I am." She flashes a smile. "But you like it."

"I do." He crooks his finger. "Let's go."

And down the hallway they disappear.

Jillian takes a sip of her drink. "Well now, this should be fun."

Chad laughs. "Indeed."

Suspicious, I stare at him. He's not... no. No way. That's impossible.

I glance longingly at the front door.

Suddenly, I want to go home.

2.

Layla

When we get to our bedroom, Michael shuts the door behind us.

I walk to the edge of our bed, anxious and excited. I had been a tiny bit bratty.

I have my reasons. Reasons Michael understands.

I'm wound up. On edge.

Michael knows this. He knows everything about me. Knows what I need and just how to give it to me.

He comes up behind me and slides his hands on my silk-covered hips, leaning his head down to brush a kiss over the curve of my neck. His erection presses against my back. "You look so fucking hot tonight."

I lean against him, arching my breasts high in the air.

We're ready to go at it. It crackles the air between us.

Since the first time I saw him it's been like this. So hot we're bound to get burned. Time has only made us stronger. Made *me* stronger. With Michael, I'm the woman I'm meant to be, and not the shell of the woman I'd become. The road had been long and hard, but I'm finally in a place where I'm free of the past. Well, almost.

It's still a dull ache, but it doesn't consume me the way it did. Doesn't run every aspect of my life.

I crane my neck and rest my head on Michael's shoulder. I'm filled with a nervous anticipation about tonight. I'm one big ball of energy; wound a couple of clicks too tight. I know the possibility of what could happen, of what he might do to me, and as much as I fear it, I need it to make me whole. To make me complete so I can erase that horrible night from my mind. So I can conquer the last of my demons.

But most important, I need to do it for Michael, because it's what he deserves. Somehow I believe it will allow me to give back a tiny portion of what he's given me. To prove that out of all the women he could have, he was right to choose me. Right to believe I'm worth all the effort he's put into me.

He reaches up and cups my breasts. "You need to be marked."

It's not a question. He knows. I have so much anxiety about tonight; I need the reminder that I belong to him.

I can already envision the fiery sting of pain on my flesh, the rise of the long, striped welt the cane will leave behind. It will hurt, and in that moment I'll hate everything about me that craves this, but after I'll feel better. Calmer. For the rest of the night, no matter what happens, I'll wear the physical reminder of his possession of me on my body. And I need that.

Part of my nerves are because tonight is the first time I've done anything like this since my fiancé was murdered before my eyes. When I met Michael I'd frequented the club I now know belongs to Brandon. It had been part of my punishment, part of my self-afflicted slide into oblivion. Since I've been with Michael we haven't been back. That place is the reminder of too much pain.

When Brandon invited us to his new club, at first I hadn't wanted to go, the memories of that horrible night too deeply engrained in my mind. Michael and I spent a lot of time talking, and in the end, we'd decided to go. This is a new place, not even really a sex club. It won't be the same. So I'm being brave, despite my memories.

In the end, it's better to face your demons so you don't drown in them.

It's time for new memories, created with the man I love more than life itself.

But it doesn't mean I'm not nervous. So I acted out, just a little bit. I need to work through all my excess energy and sassy is the way I do it.

Michael doesn't let it slide. Doesn't always give me what I want. But tonight he understands I need the pain to ground me. And he's not going to deny me.

He runs his hands over my nipples, rubbing his thumbs back and forth until I moan. I'm not wearing a bra, or panties. My dress is really little more than a nightgown. The white the only concession I'd made for the angelic theme. His fingers trail over my ribs, down my stomach, before bunching the fabric and raising the hem above my hips. He slips between my legs where I'm already wet and aching.

He growls, and bites my neck. "So goddamn beautiful. So goddamn wet."

I groan and arch into his touch. He's skilled, driving me crazy but never delivering the type of pressure I need to get close to orgasm. A slow, delicious tease. His thumb brushes my clit. I sigh his name. "Michael."

"Mine." His free hand wraps around my neck, his fingers squeezing just enough to set my heart racing into overdrive.

"Yes."

"Should I fuck you now, or later?"

"Both," I gasp. Losing myself in him.

"Greedy." His pressure increases, and I lean against him, letting him take all my weight so I don't have to think about anything but his hands on my body.

"Always," I whisper. Because I am. I know how lucky I am and don't ever take it for granted.

As I sit on the sharp edge of coming, he stops. The silk of

my dress slides down my thighs, and his hand leaves my neck to press against the base of my spine. He exerts pressure. "Down you go."

I don't hesitate, I just lean down over the edge of the bed, my arms resting on the soft comforter, my face turned, eyes closed.

He moves, and I don't have to look to know he's going to the wardrobe in the corner that contains various toys and instruments he sometimes uses on me. We're a hands on type of couple, but there's always exceptions, and the cane is one of them. The door opens and there's the sound of shifting objects before he closes it again.

I gulp. Swallow hard. And hold my breath.

I hate the cane as much as I love it.

Unless you're a girl like me, it's hard to explain how you can love something and hate something in equal measure. How it can be terrifying and make you drip with excitement.

You'll just have to trust me.

Without a word he slides my dress up past the curve of my ass and trails the bamboo across my skin.

I shiver. In lust and in fear.

"Is this what you were hoping for with your sassy attitude?" He slides the cane along the side of bare leg, over my thighs, down my calf and up again.

"No."

"Do you still think I'm being unreasonable?"

"Yes." Clearly I'm not the smartest girl.

He laughs, and squeezes my hip hard enough I'll have a bruise tomorrow. "I am, a little, you've been much brattier. But I want to hurt you."

I shudder and a trickle of wetness slides down my thigh.

"I want to mark you and you want to be marked."

"Yes." I struggle for breath and clutch the comforter.

"Two strikes. I think that will be a proper reminder, don't you?"

"I do." It's more than enough. Just enough. I've taken more, but we are going out. It's a reminder, not a real punishment.

He steps away from me and I keep my eyes tightly shut.

"Raise up on your elbows."

I comply, shaking my head so my chestnut hair curls down my back, and around my shoulders, creating a sight I know he'll enjoy.

"Very pretty," he says from behind me and by the sound of his voice, he's lined up. "You ready?"

"Yes." I try and relax. It's so much easier if you relax.

But when you're waiting for pain, sometimes relaxation is too great a goal.

Muscles tense, I hold my breath.

I wait.

And wait.

And wait.

Finally, I hear it, the whisper through the air a fraction of a second before it strikes my skin.

I cry out, falling out of position, unable to help the scream as the fiery sting explodes, sharp and intensely focused.

"Back in position, girl." His tone is that hard, commanding bark I love more than anything.

I hurry back into place, and brace myself, but this time there's no waiting, and the second I'm anchored he hits me again.

The pain brings tears to my eyes and I squeeze them shut as I count to ten. I can already feel the two distinct stripes running across my ass, can feel the rise of welts that will be white before they turn red.

It hurts. A lot.

But the tension that had bound me up so tight before is gone and I feel fresh and new. Accomplished somehow. All that's left behind is insatiable lust.

Michael puts the cane on the bed, and soothes a hand over my back. "Better?"

I nod. Still taking deep breaths through the fiery pain.

"What do you need?" His is tone gruff.

"You." He's all I ever need.

He grips my hair and twists so my head cranes back. "Fucking gorgeous." Then he covers my mouth, claiming me in that way only he can.

His tongue strokes, tangling with mine. Possessing me so I feel nothing but his lips, and the brand of his ownership in the two stripes of fire along my skin.

He pulls away, and says against my mouth, "Hard and fast, Layla."

I arch my back, moaning my acceptance.

He moves behind me, and I hear the zipper slide down, before he grips my hips.

He kicks my legs farther apart and then slams home.

I cry out as he fills me to the hilt and his skin abrades the marks he's left behind.

He pulls out and thrusts back in and my clit brushes against the edge of the bed.

Every single ebb and surge is heaven. Every rub of his hip against the marks he left increases my desire. So good. So goddamn good I might lose my mind.

It's all I can think as he fucks me, hard and rough, taking complete control.

Filling me up. Making me whole.

The orgasm barrels down on me and I gasp his name in a pleading question. "Michael?"

He growls, and impossibly increases his pace. "Yes, Layla."

I explode around him. Pleasure mixes with pain, creating a kaleidoscope of sensation that crests through my body in pummeling waves, making me mindless and incoherent.

He follows me, spilling inside me over and over again until we're both breathless. Normally he'd collapse on top of me, but he doesn't, conscious of the marks on my skin. Besides, we have guests waiting for us to come back so we can go on what is sure to be a strange adventure.

He pulls out and helps me to my feet, my knees still wobbly.

My dress falls effortlessly back in place. After he's zipped up, he twines his hand around my neck. "Better?"

"Yes."

He kisses me, soft and sure. "I love you, Layla."

"I love you too." More than he can possibly know, possibly understand. I rise to my tiptoes, twining my arms around his neck. "Thank you."

"You're welcome." He licks my pounding pulse. "You'll be okay, sugar."

"I know." I squeeze him one more time before I let him go.

He leads me back into the living room, hand clasped with mine.

When we get there, Jillian, winces at me. "You okay?"

"I'm great." A smile graces my lips, wide and open. Because, I am.

Leo laughs. "All sorted out, girl?"

I wrinkle my nose at him. "Are we ready to go?"

Jillian winks. "We were waiting on you guys."

"Well, I'm ready."

I turn to Ruby, who's standing next to Chad. They look odd together—my rocker, Snow White best friend and Chad, who is about as clean cut as can be. She seems to have no clue that Chad is also dominant, and I've thought about clueing her in, but Michael insists she should figure it out on her own. So that's what I've done. Time will tell if it's a wise decision or not.

Ruby's brow is furrowed and she looks distressed. Which she probably is. I'll have to talk to her later and try and explain.

I'd debated inviting her to this party, because it's out of her comfort zone, but in the end, I gave her the option and let her make up her mind. She's curious about domination and submission, despite all the times she tells me she can't figure out why I'd want such a thing.

All her protests that she'd never let a man control her ear... telling. She asks too many questions, watches Michael and Leo a little bit too closely, and is a little too interested for casual curiosity. So I'm giving her a vehicle to find out more, but she'll have to pick up the keys and start the ignition.

She'll get an eyeful. Tonight, subtle isn't an option.

4.

Ruby

I'm nervous as we walk to the place, unsure what to expect. Located in downtown Chicago, Brandon's club is off the beaten path, which should work against its success, but from what I understand he has some sort of Midas touch when it comes to business, and considering the current buzz, this place will be no different. As we walk through a near deserted area, Chad walks next to me and I bite my lip.

He takes my hand and squeezes, and when I look up at him, he smiles. "You okay, Ruby?"

I dart a nervous glance at the rest of the group. He spoke low and I don't think they heard anything. I nod. "I'm good."

He drops my hand but stays close to my side. He's considerate that way. My dad would love him. He's a real stickler for manners and gentlemanly like behavior.

My dad hates my type of guy. Not that I've brought anyone home.

We veer off onto a little sub block, walking against the

sharp Chicago winter wind before we come to a nondescript, loft building with a locked door.

Layla told me he'd modeled it after a prohibition speakeasy. But right now it looks like an abandoned building. Come tomorrow night there will be a line down the block, but tonight is a private, intimate party for Brandon's inner circle.

A slot in the door slides open and two eyes peer out, Michael gives his name, and a second later the lock clicks and we're shown inside.

Even though I'm only here as an observer my heart still thumps too loud in my chest as an attendant takes our coats. It's like I've caught the excitement of Jillian and Layla, and combined it with my own personal brand of nervous energy. I've never been to a sex party and I can't even begin to imagine what I'll encounter. We walk down a corridor that leads to another closed door with a bouncer standing in front of it.

The guy is huge, with muscles the size of my thighs and tats running the length of his arms. His massive chest stretches the confines of his black T-shirt. While he doesn't look particularly old, his hair is salt-and-pepper and his eyes are so blue they appear electric.

He looks like a badass. Like ex-military.

He nods at Michael. "Brandon will be here in a minute."

Jillian laughs. "Is this Brandon or what? It's like the freakin' Pentagon to get in."

The bouncer gives her a raised brow that makes the fine hair on the nape of my neck stand up.

Leo slides a hand around her waist. "She's a little high strung tonight."

The guy flashes a grin. "Good luck with that."

Leo kisses the side of Jillian's neck. "Come to the back room later, I'll have her on display."

Jillian sucks in her breath.

Michael shakes his head. "For fuck's sake, this is a nightmare."

The guy looks at Michael before shifting his attention to Jillian, giving her a thorough once over. "She's very hot."

Michael looks like he's grinding his teeth. "She's my sister."

The bouncer shrugs. "Still hot." He turns to Layla and gives her a long, slow perusal. "Not that you're suffering in that department."

Layla beams at him and does a little curtsey. "Why thank you, kind sir."

He winks at her. "Aren't you a good girl?"

"Always." The sweet compliance in Layla's voice could rival the saints in heaven.

Michael palms her ass and Layla sucks in a breath, her expression twisting a bit. "Don't let her fool you, she only looks like an angel."

The guy laughs and it's like smoke, a sexy, husky sound. "And what trouble are you going to get into, little girl?"

Layla bats her eyelashes. "Who me? I never get into trouble."

Oh my god, she's actually flirting with him. And Michael's just standing there, clearly amused.

The door opens and Brandon walks out, wearing his dimpled grin, and black. He's blond, tall, lanky and gorgeous. Jillian once said he looked like a young Matthew McConaughey in *True Detective*, and it's an accurate description. "Sorry to keep you waiting."

Apparently black is the only acceptable attire for a man tonight. Except for Chad, who's dressed for casual Friday.

Michael juts a chin at the bouncer. "No worries, your man here is keeping us entertained by flirting with Layla."

Brandon thumps the bouncer on the back. "Well, Hunter has excellent taste in women."

I frown. Hunter hasn't even glanced in my direction.

I'm like a wallflower here. I'm not sure I like the role.

We start filing into the room and Hunter nods at Jillian. "I'll be seeing you later."

Jillian blushes while everyone else laughs, and I just stand there feeling lost and confused.

Suddenly there's a hand on my waist, and I jerk back in surprise. It's Chad. His brow is furrowed, looking at me in an intense, searching way. "Are you sure you're okay, you seem a little off?"

"I'm good," I say, making my words as light as possible. How does he keep doing that? Reading me? I don't like it.

He rubs a hand up my spine. It's not sexual, it's more friendly, reassuring. "Don't be afraid to let us know if you get overwhelmed."

Puzzled, I blink at him, and again I get that strange sense he might be bent the same way as Leo and Michael. But that has to be wrong. I smile, wanting to be on even ground with them, or at least with him. "I went to that Metal Punk bar that just opened in Wicker Park, if I can handle that, I can handle anything."

He flashes me a grin. "Watching people thrash is a bit different than watching people have sex."

The moment of awareness flashes, then recedes, and I'm left looking into his friendly face. He really is a good guy. He's just making sure I'm okay. We start to walk, and I bump his hip with mine. "Thanks."

"Your welcome."

"You're a regular Boy Scout, aren't you?"

He laughs. "Yep. Ask anyone."

"What are you even doing here?" I ask, but as soon as I enter the space everything else, including his answer, fades into the background.

Holy Shit.

I had no idea what I'd been expecting but it wasn't this. I think, in my head, I'd pictured something small and seedy, with all sorts of… devices that make me shudder whenever I run across them on the Internet.

"Wow." My voice is awed, because this place is spectacular.

Brandon named the club The Lair and it was a perfect fit, because that's exactly what it felt like. It's rich, and intricate. Like being in a castle. The lighting casts everything in a dim, moody golden glow. I can't even begin to guess how high the ceilings are but they seem to almost disappear into the sky. The woodwork is thick, mahogany and intricately carved. The furniture looks like it came out of an eighteen-century French boudoir and drawing room. All dark wood, antiqued, and red velvet.

It's the most gorgeous, most decadent place I've ever been in.

It looks like a huge sitting room, with arrangements of chairs and tables clustered together to create an intimate setting. The only homage it pays to being an establishment is the massive bar that lines one wall, but even that looks like it came from another century.

The room is already filled with people but it's a comfortable-sized crowd. Not packed like a bar or club. I am too stunned by the décor, and sheer awesomeness of the place, to be preoccupied by the patrons nestled into the nooks and crannies.

Jillian whistles. "I saw it being built, but seriously, you've outdone yourself, Brandon."

"It's gorgeous," Layla agrees.

Brandon holds his arms wide. "Not sure the grandparents would agree with how I'm spending my trust fund, but I like it."

"What's not to like," I say, still studying the intricate scrollwork on the wood.

Brandon walks over and kisses me on each cheek. "The lovely Ruby decided to come tonight. I'm honored."

That's the way Brandon is, he makes everyone feel welcome, even when they don't belong.

I stand on my tiptoes and hug him. "This is the prettiest place I've ever seen."

He laughs, kisses me again, this time on the lips, and says, "Is that a compliment?"

"It is." I pull away and I walk over to the wall to touch the wood "Where did you get this?"

"A Parisian Catholic church," Brandon says.

Layla laughs. "You are so perverse."

It takes me a second for her meaning to dawn on me. Blessed wood in a place that will host sex parties. It is an odd sense of humor.

Brandon walks to Layla and wraps his arms around her. "And don't you forget it."

He stands back, grasps her hands and holds out her arms so he could see her. "My, my, my you're looking good enough to eat, darling girl."

Layla smiles. "Thank you."

Brandon's blue eyes twinkle with amusement. "It's nights like these, when I can see how hard your nipples are, that I wish Michael wasn't so possessive of you."

Michael shakes his head and Layla bats him in the chest. "Whatever."

Brandon turns a sly glance to Michael. "Any chance you're feeling flexible tonight?"

Michael rolls his eyes. "Not even a little bit."

Brandon sighs and turns to Jillian. "And there's my favorite girl." He kisses her too on the cheek. "Aren't you looking like a little dominatrix this evening?"

Jillian is tall, like a warrior princess, there's not much that doesn't make her look like a dominatrix. She winks. "Only on the outside."

Brandon cocks a brow and gives her a long look. "Oh, I know what a slut you are on the inside."

"Christ," Michael mutters.

I suck in a gasp of shock.

Jillian's fiancé chuckles.

I'm so confused. How can Leo laugh? Leo didn't even look the least bit perturbed that Brandon just called his future wife a slut. In fact, he looks kind of pleased.

Brandon shakes Leo's hand and they pat each other in that guy hug way.

I feel as though I've just tumbled down the rabbit's hole into some sort of bizarre alternate universe.

Brandon gives Jillian a smirk before saying to Leo, "I have the room all ready for her."

Leo gives Jillian a stern-jawed once over. "Good."

Jillian appears as though she might drop into a dead faint.

Brandon turns to Michael. "And before we fill up, is there anything you have in mind for the lovely Layla?"

Michael crosses his arm and raises a brow at Layla. "Well, sugar?"

Layla loses her sassy smile, gulps and looks away, shaking her head.

I wonder if she's thinking about John. The last time she was in a club like this with him. The night he was murdered.

"You sure about that?" Michael is talking to her in that way he has, all hard command.

I fight my urge to run to her rescue. It wasn't so long ago that my best friend was so fragile and broken I worried if she'd kill herself. She's never said it, but I suspect there were times she contemplated ending her misery.

When you've seen your best friend go through something so horrific, it's hard not to be overprotective. And that's the hardest thing for me about seeing Michael with Layla. He does not treat her with kid gloves. While the logical part of me understands that's what she needs and desires, the part that watched her struggle to get through the day for eighteen months is not as sympathetic.

She licks her lips. "I'm good."

Michael peers at her. "There's not something you need?"

She shakes her head again.

He walks over and curls his hand around her neck. "You need to ask for it, Layla."

I open my mouth, unable to watch him badger her anymore, but then Chad grips my wrist and squeezes hard enough I'm stunned. I jerk my head to glare at him.

He shakes his head, signaling me to be quiet.

Who does he think he is?

I'm about to ignore him and demand Michael stop, but then I realize everyone is very quiet and still, and there's a hush through our small group. Everyone grasped some significance about the interaction between Michael and Layla but me.

That I'm once again left out of this whole other part of my

best friend's life.

Layla grips Michael's shirt and shakes her head.

With his thumb under her chin, he forces her to meet his gaze. "You want to ask, all you need to do is say the words and I'll give you what you need." He kisses her. "What you've been craving."

She takes a stuttery breath.

Why do they all understand? Even Chad seems to understand.

I grit my teeth and blink against the tightness in my throat.

Layla opens her mouth, closes it, and then opens it again.

I watch the struggle play out across her beautiful features.

The conflict in her gaze.

The indecision in the set of her jaw.

The need to escape in her fluttery breath.

So why, if she feels all those things, does she do this? What drives her? I can't understand and can't deny it makes me uncomfortable.

She clutches at the fabric of his shirt, but he doesn't seem to notice. No, he just watches her in that patient way he has, his thumb gently caressing the line of her throat.

No one says a word.

They all just stand and wait.

Her thickly made up lashes flutter. "Will I disappoint you… if I can't?"

She trails off, unable to finish what she was going to say.

I clench my hands into fists, if he says yes, I will kill him.

But instead, his face softens and he brushes her lips with his own. "Not even a little bit."

The sincerity of his words, the look of love and utter devotion on his face, makes my heart squeeze.

I have never had anyone look at me like that. Not even close.

"Are you sure?" Her voice is a tremble.

"Have I ever lied to you?"

She shakes her head.

"It's your choice, girl. I'm proud of you no matter what."

This seems to lighten something in her, and she changes from the nervous creature she'd been, to something beautiful. Transforms like a butterfly before my very eyes. She takes a deep breath and straightens her shoulders. "I'm ready."

"And what are you ready for?" Michael asks.

She looks him right in the eyes. "I want you to tie me up."

Shock rolls through me. Layla told me once she'd never let anyone bind her in any way. That she couldn't handle it. Her attackers had tied her up and she said she'd never feel safe that way again.

That she is asking this from Michael astounds me.

"Are you sure?" His voice is calm, his expression steady.

"Positive." She nods in further affirmation.

"Good girl." He turns to Brandon. "I assume you have something in mind?"

Brandon walks over to Layla and gives her a look so tender my eyes fill with tears. Then he tucks a lock of her hair behind her ear. "I know just the thing."

She lowers her gaze. "I trust you."

Michael slides his arm around her and kisses her temple. "But first, a drink." He squeezes Layla's hip. "One drink for now, but you can have as many as you want later."

Layla beams up at him, not seeming the least bit perturbed her boyfriend just told her how many drinks she could have.

Brandon waves them to a corner and starts walking in that direction. "I reserved a spot."

These people—they know Layla now—better than me. They know a whole part of her that eludes me. I feel separate from her, and I don't like it. I resist the urge to scream like a petulant child, *She's my best friend you can't have her.* It's petty, and wrong, but I don't know how to stop feeling the way I do. How to stop the jealousy that eats away at me. It wasn't like that when John was alive. He was a part of us, our group. Now Layla's a part of something else and I'm tagging along, like a square peg in a round hole.

And, well, it's just… I used to be Layla's rock.

It hurts that I'm not anymore.

I start to walk in the direction they're heading, but once again Chad grips my elbow. I turn around to look at him. "What's wrong?"

He studies me for a long time and I have to resist the urge to shift under his gaze. Finally, he says to me, "Since you've never been to something like this before, you should probably understand the ground rules."

"Ground rules?"

He nods. "Yes, there are rules, and I can tell they're all preoccupied and didn't think to cue you in."

"What are you talking about?" I thought tonight had no rules.

He crosses his arms over his chest and momentarily it occurs to me how broad shouldered he is, but that's forgotten as soon as he speaks. "Don't interrupt when a dominant is talking to his submissive, no matter what it looks like to you or how little you understand. Brandon's got people monitoring everything, so if things get out of hand, his people will take care of it."

Defensiveness stirs in my chest and I repress the desire to snap at him. The guy doesn't know he's pushing all my buttons, playing on my fears that I'm no longer part of Layla's life. I peer up at him. "What would you know about it?"

He sighs. "I can't believe you're still asking that question."

"You've lost me, Beaver." I call him Beaver sometimes, like *Leave it to Beaver* because he's so good.

He drags a hand through his hair. "I really can't figure out if you're being deliberately dense."

Nerves skitter across my skin as I have that sudden awareness again that I'm missing something key about Chad. But I put on a good show, laughing as I wave at the retreating couples. "What? Are you trying to say you're like them?"

He tilts his head. "Why do you find that hard to believe?"

"Look at how sweet and innocent you are."

Suddenly his expression hardens, and it firms his jaw, putting a glint in his eye. "Honey, the only babe in the woods here is you."

5.

Layla

I shift restlessly in my seat, my fingers playing over the stem of my wine glass. A special Bordeaux Brandon has saved for us. But I can't enjoy it.

Next to me, Michael puts his hand on my leg and whispers in my ear, "Just breathe, Layla. That's all you have to do is take one breath at a time, relax and enjoy yourself."

I nod, trying to pay attention to the calm sound of his voice.

This is a huge thing for me. As he well knows.

It's why he's made me ask for it.

He makes me ask for everything big. After the first time the decision will be out of my hands, but that first time it's entirely my choice.

Being tied up is something I'd sworn I'd never do again. Michael uses his hands to restrain me, I've at least managed that much, but I've yet to take that final step. I'd known it was coming. It was something we'd talked a lot about, but when I was up against the decision, the inevitability, I faltered.

Michael tucks a crooked finger under my chin and tilts my head to look at him. "Hey, it's just going to be you and me. Nobody else. You don't have to worry about putting on a performance. You don't have to worry about disappointing me. Or if you need to stop. All you need to worry about is you and me. Understood?"

The knot in my stomach loosens and I realize I was worried about just this, and didn't know it. But of course, Michael knew. He always knows. I bite my lip. "You won't let anyone watch?"

"No." He kisses me. "It's just you and me. In a private room upstairs. And if you panic, we'll stop, and try again some other day."

My eyes go misty. "What did I do to deserve you?"

He cracks a grin. "You must have been a very good girl in another life."

"Indeed." I give him a smile meant only for him. "Thank you."

He shakes his head. "No, thank you. I know this is important to you, and I want you to have it. But don't make it a pass / fail thing like your overachiever brain is prone to do. It's a process."

I nod. I know what he's saying. I'm hard on myself. Too hard.

I've come to believe taking this step with Michael is essential to my healing process as I claim back the woman I was before fate and death stole it all away from me.

I want this, because I want to take back what those men stole from me.

But Michael is right; I've made it huge in my brain. Of epic significance.

I pick up my glass and take a sip of wine. I want to recapture my mood from earlier. That sassy girl living on the edge of danger. She's there, lurking below the surface, ready to make her appearance. I just have to unwind a bit.

I take a deep breath, and relax against Michael. We're on a

two-person couch and he puts his arm around me and pushes me back. He twists, leans over me, blocking me from view of the others, before pressing his hand between my bare thighs.

He kisses me, long and deep, his fingers digging into my skin.

I wrap my arms around him, getting lost in the feel of him. His tongue strokes mine as his thumb plays over my inner thigh.

He pulls away and says against my lips, "If my sister weren't here, I'd fuck you with my fingers until you screamed."

I moan and arch. She's not my sister. I don't care.

He bites my neck then pulls away, adjusting us on the couch.

Jillian grins at us, and shrugs. "I could just turn away."

Michael says, "Shut up, Jillian."

At the exact same time I say, "All right."

Leo laughs. "God, this is fun when your own relatives aren't involved."

"Fuck you," Michael says, his tone good-natured. He pinches me with no real force, his expression amused. "Behave."

See, I'm already feeling better. That's the one thing I've learned since I've been with Michael. To roll with my emotions, no matter how much they irritate me. Like all things in life, once you give up the struggle, things get a lot less complicated.

Ruby walks up to the table, looking vaguely uneasy. Chad is behind her. I smile and she gives me a halfhearted smile in return.

I'm not sure I made the right decision asking her to come. She seems out of sorts and unhappy.

Not at all like her normal funny, sarcastic self.

I need to get her alone to talk to her, to make sure she's all right. I frown and say, "You want to go to the bathroom?"

I expect her to jump at the offer, but she shakes her head and says quietly, "I'm good."

Jillian however, does bound up. "I'll go."

I give Michael a quick kiss and grab my bag. I look at Ruby. "Are you sure you don't want to come with us?"

Her expression tightens and she glances away to the open space behind me. "Maybe later."

I want to press, but turn to Michael. He gives me a smile. "We'll take care of her."

I shift my attention back to Ruby. But she's not paying attention, her face is remote and unreadable, but I know something is bothering her.

All I can hope is that I didn't make a mistake. And that, at some point, she'll find the courage to talk to me.

Jillian

Layla and I hook arms and head off to the ladies' room.

We are causing quite a stir and as we pass, I can't help but notice the men turning to look at us, their gazes hungry. We really do look like an angel and a devil, only you know, slutty.

Brandon comes up behind us and puts his arms around our waists. "Come with me, you can use my private bathroom."

I laugh up at him, and bat my lashes. "I feel so special."

"That's because you are special, baby doll."

Brandon calls me baby doll and Layla darling girl.

In case you were keeping track.

He leads us into an office, befitting of the millionaire he is, with dark wood, and a huge desk that has to be an antique. Brandon pretends to be all modern, but I suspect he's secretly a Renaissance man, in love with all things old and beautiful. I can relate.

I'm getting my master's degree in fine art with an emphasis on that period, so I recognize the signs. When I'm through with school I'm going to become an art dealer, and have already started making contacts in the business. When Brandon was decorating the place I went with him to galleries all over the city and I couldn't help but notice he was attracted to the classics. With an edge, of course.

Behind the desk is a huge oil painting we found on one of our trips by an obscure French artist. I gasp in pleasure when I see it, absolutely floored by its beauty. I forget the bathroom and run over to it and stroke my fingers over the intricate black-and-patina scrolled frame. "Wow. Brandon, the space is perfect, it's even more spectacular than I remember."

"It is. Thank you for convincing me it was exactly right," Brandon says from behind me.

"Who's the artist?" Layla asks.

"Gaston Lamar." I stand back to marvel at the work in its entirety. It's a nude, of a woman on a chaise, her lover in dark shadows. The only thing visible is his strong hand entwined over the delicate cords of her throat. She's looking at him, her expression full of rapture and just a hint of fear. As soon as I saw the piece hanging there I'd known it was perfect. Not only did it have a distinct Dom/sub vibe, I wanted to sit there and stare at it for hours.

That's how I always know a piece is good. When I don't want to look away. When I want to get lost in its beauty. When I think about it throughout my day, longing to see it again.

"Why did you need convincing?" Layla asked, and I can hear the awe in her voice. "It's stunning."

Brandon chuckles and I finally tear myself away from the piece.

I roll my eyes at Layla. "He wanted vintage pornography."

Layla raises a brow. "This is better."

"Of course it is," I say, flipping my hair.

Brandon shrugs one shoulder. "When I'm wrong, I'm wrong. I had a vision of what I wanted, but when it comes to art, Jillian is always right."

I wag my finger at him. "And don't you forget it."

Brandon grins at me. "Baby doll, you did get paid."

I did. Quite well. For the very first time I'd been paid for real art dealer work. When I got the check, I'd been like a little kid, dancing around the condo I share with Leo like a lunatic, screaming in delight while Leo grinned at me, completely amused by my antics.

I don't believe in hiding my emotions.

Of course, I could have done something practical with the money, like invest it, but that's not really my style. I have plenty of time to save, but this was special so I'd taken my fiancé away for a long weekend in Mexico and paid for the whole thing, much to Leo's pretend griping.

I wink at Brandon. "I'm worth every penny."

"That you are." Brandon straightens and sighs. "I've got to get back to it, you girls be good in here."

"We will," Layla and I parroted at the same time.

He narrows his eyes. "I don't trust you."

Layla did her sweet, innocent act on him. "I'm always good."

"Me too," I say, mimicking her tone.

Brandon shakes his head. "You're little deviants."

We laugh and he takes his leave, closing the door behind us.

We take turns in the bathroom, but then instead of going back to the main bar we plop down on Brandon's brown leather furniture. Furniture that's clearly designed for fucking, with all its curved lines, and interesting angles. Layla points again to the picture. "You've really outdone yourself."

"Isn't it gorgeous? Is it wrong that I kind of want to steal it?"

Layla laughs. "I'll help."

We grin at each other, and then Layla glances toward the door and a cloud passes over her face. She clears her throat. "Do you think I was wrong to invite Ruby?"

I've always liked Layla's best friend. Although the two women couldn't be more opposite. Layla is stunning in a very classical way. The art masters would have had a field day with her. She's also traditional. Ruby, on the other hand, is a gorgeous little rocker girl that, from what I understand from

Layla, wants no part of mainstream life.

Whenever we've gone out as a group, it's always been in regular circumstances, normal dinners, dancing, bar hopping and the like. Circumstances where Leo and Michael aren't in your face about their dominant natures. This is the first time where all our depravity is right out there for the world to see.

Ruby is uncomfortable. That's obvious. I hadn't missed that she wanted to interrupt the interplay between Michael and Layla, or that she hadn't liked what she'd witnessed. I saw Chad stop her. I understood she hadn't realized what was really going on between them, but to me, it had seemed clear it hadn't been bad.

I run my hand over the leather couch. "I don't know. Why'd you bring her?"

Layla shakes her head, blowing out a breath. "I think she's curious, more than curious actually."

My eyes widen. That's not a vibe I'd picked up on, but on the other hand, she'd agreed to come along. "Why do you think that?"

"The questions she asks. The way she watches Michael and Leo. Michael says she'll need to figure it out on her own, and maybe I'm projecting. Assigning meaning when there isn't one. I don't know."

I wrinkle my nose, remembering those first conversations with Leo about what he was, that now seem a lifetime ago. He'd told me I had to figure things out on my own. "Leo said something similar to me once, and it didn't go over well. Sometimes you need a little more of a push. Have you tried talking to her?"

Layla nods. "Yeah, a couple times, but she insists she can't imagine why I'd ever let a man do that to me. So there's not much I can do."

I use to think that. I shudder. Thinking of this morning, moaning and panting over Leo's knee. I was wrong.

But that doesn't mean that Ruby is wrong too. I narrow my eyes. "Why does it matter? Do you care if she's into the same things you are?"

Layla shakes her head. "God no. Of course not. I never even told her about John and me, and never thought about it. We'd never even talked about it until Michael. But the more I open up, the more I explain, the more questions she asks. And right now, she just seems... unhappy. Distant." Layla runs her hands through her hair. "Maybe I'm suffering from role reversal. I'm used to being the difficult, distant one while she's trying to get me to talk. Maybe that's all it is."

"Maybe," I say, before smiling. "But maybe not."

Layla glances at the door, as though she's afraid someone might come in, and then lowers her voice. "Sometimes I catch her watching Michael and me." Layla bites her lower lip. "And, well, I think I see jealousy there."

I can understand that. I can't deny there is something about my brother and Layla. Something captivating. When they walk into a room, eyes linger on them. I smile. "When I was single, I would have been insanely jealous of you and Michael too."

Layla shrugs. "I don't want her jealous. I want her happy."

"And you think some man dominating her will make her happy?"

"No, I'm not saying that." She blows out a hard breath. "I just sense something."

I raise a brow. "Is that why Chad's here?"

Layla laughs. "No! Can you even imagine?"

"Nope." I can't. They are polar opposites. While Ruby looks like a renegade, there's something almost restrained about her. In contrast, Chad looks all American and clean cut, but I've seen the guy work it, and he's as dominant as they come.

Layla continues, "Chad's here because he's our friend, he's part of our little group now. I'm not worried about him. He knows who he is. And, yes, his taste in women might be a little easy for him without the challenge I think he needs, but that's his business. Ruby is mine."

"I get it. If Gwen were unhappy, I'd want to help her too." Gwen Johnson has been my best friend since we were a year old; there isn't anything I wouldn't do for her. And I do mean anything. I'd move heaven and earth for her if it was in my power. "So what do you think we should do?"

"What can we do?" Layla holds up her hands as though in surrender.

I grin. "At bare minimum we can show her why you'd want a man controlling you."

She grins back. "That's true. We can show her that, at least until we go into our separate corners."

"Exactly." At the thought of tonight's events I shiver with lust. I've already let the nerves slip away for the time being, because I'm beyond excited. And I trust Leo implicitly. He's been whispering the most depraved things into my ear, sliding his fingers up my legs, commenting on how I'm such a little slut with my drenched thighs.

And it's just making me hotter. Wetter.

Once I get to wherever he puts me, I'll be nervous, but for now I'm just letting that fevered pitch take over. Because there's nothing more I love than that place I go where all sanity shuts off and I'm riding on a wave of blissful, endless ecstasy.

"Perfect," Layla says. A sly expression slides over her features and she glances toward the door before leaning forward on her chair. "I think we should have a little fun, don't you?"

I giggle. I so love devious Layla. "Oh yes."

"I don't know about you, but I've been really put through the paces today."

We don't talk details, because of Michael and mine's unfortunate sibling relationship, but Layla is the only submissive friend I have. And I know from talking to her, that I'm the same for her. She's the only person who understands, that I can talk to about these things, and I'm so grateful to have her in my life. So I just try not to think too much about the fact that it's my brother that's the orchestrator of her madness.

"Me too." I puff out my lip in a pout. "It's really not fair."

"It certainly is not." Layla tilts her head and her hair flows over her shoulder. "I think it's only fair we twist the knife a bit, you know, put on a little show for them."

A huge smile spreads over my lips. "Michael is going to hate that."

Layla's features twist into exaggerated sympathy. "Awww, poor baby."

I roar with laughter. "Let's go."

This is going to be so fun.

7.

Ruby

I sit at the table as the three guys talk around me, all apparently in a hell of a good mood.

The only person not having a good time is me.

I'm still reeling from Chad's revelation. I mean, how can that be? Him of all people? Leo and Michael I get—they have a way about them—but Chad is just an affable, good guy.

How did I end up the only straight-laced person here?

"Ruby?" A male voice rips me from my thoughts.

I blink, finding Michael, Leo and Chad staring at me. I've missed something. I frown. "Sorry?"

Chad points at the waitress, a pretty brunette dressed as an angel in all white. "Do you want something to drink?"

I wish I had someone monitoring my drinks. I blink again. Where did that come from? I want no such thing. I don't want anyone telling me what to do. Ever.

So why did that thought pop into my head? It must be the care in the act. Because I can't remember the last guy that even opened the door for me.

That must be it.

It's the care, not the intent.

In a flash of memory, I see my dad, sitting at the table reading his paper, while my mom bustled around him like a happy, little homemaker. It had made me ill. She could have been so much more. Once she'd been a promising violinist, but she'd abandoned all that for my dad.

She'd given up her dreams. Her goals. Her life. So she could do his bidding.

I was not that kind of girl.

"Ruby?" Chad says again. "She's waiting."

The girl flutters her lashes at him and gives him a coy, flirty look.

Something thuds in my chest. Something I don't like and refuse to name.

I clear my throat. "Vodka soda, please."

"Coming right up." The angel girl bites her lip and looks at Chad. "My break's in a couple hours."

Chad grins at her. "I'm sure you'll find me if you need something."

"Oh, I will." Her tone so full of seduction I have a sudden urge to punch her.

How does she know he's not my date? That I'm not a contender?

She gives him a hungry once over before turning with a swish of her hips, sashaying off with an exaggerated sway for Chad's benefit.

That knot sits in my stomach and I pick up a napkin and twist it. I shouldn't have come. I'm not in the right frame of mind. Instead of something fun and interesting that will appease my curiosity, I'm suffering from a mess of emotions that confuse me.

Maybe I should make up an excuse and go home.

But I can't do that, Layla will insist on following me and I can't ruin her night. I know how much she's looking forward to this.

I'll slip away when she goes to the private room Brandon arranged for Michael and Layla.

With an escape planned, the tension in my shoulders eases and I blow out a slow breath.

Leo raises a brow at Chad. "She looks promising."

Chad shrugs, but doesn't say anything.

"You can ask Brandon what she's into, he'll know," Leo says.

Chad turns his gaze to where the waitress is leaning over the bar, working at the computer. "If I'm interested, I'll find out myself."

That queasiness settles in my throat.

I'm not jealous.

I mean, why would I be jealous? I'm not attracted to Chad. But I find that I'm… well, I don't know what I am. I just had it in my head he'd be the odd man out with me. That while the couples went off and did their kinky things, we'd sit in the corner, drink and have a good laugh at all this nonsense. But it turns out, with the dark-haired bombshell waitress, I could end up sitting here alone.

The notion makes me even more determined to slip out the second Layla and Michael go off for their private escapade.

And speak of the devil.

Layla and Jillian emerge from the crowd now littering the floor, swaying to the music thumping loud over the speakers.

They look exactly right. Exactly like they belong.

Like sex and sin.

Heaven and hell.

People part for them; men stop what they are doing and stare after them, a look of stunned awe on their faces.

I swallow hard.

Michael shakes his head. "That's trouble."

"Agreed," Leo says, his voice amused, but his dark eyes are on Jillian. Hot and possessive.

"What's it going to be? Should we get them in line now? Or later." Michael scrubs a hand over his jaw.

"Later. Let's see what kind of rope they hang themselves

with," Leo says.

Michael nods. "Agreed."

A man tries to stop Layla, his hand encircling her wrist. She shakes her head and points to the necklace around her throat, a fine, delicate silver chain with a lock and key hanging off it. After all this time the significance of the charm finally registers in my brain. It's a symbol of ownership. The man nods, and promptly removes his hands.

He gives Jillian the eye, but she flashes her engagement ring, before pointing at the table. At Leo.

The man looks over at us, grins, and raises his glass in a toast.

Leo chuckles. "I almost feel sorry for him." He crooks his finger at Jillian. "Almost."

Layla and Jillian continue their slow strut across the room, their hips a provocative sway, their breasts thrust out.

Brandon comes up to the table, props himself up against the couch, and whistles. "Good luck with that."

Michael and Leo grin at each other.

Layla and Jillian stop in front of their men and plop their evening bags on the table. Layla licks her lips, a sly expression on her face. She's slicked her mouth with some sort of crimson gloss. She tilts her head toward the dance floor. "Jillian and I want to dance."

Michael's gaze cruises over her body. "Are you going to be a good girl?"

"Of course."

He nods. "All right then."

Now it's Jillian's turn and she looks at Leo, the question in her eyes.

He looks right back, saying nothing.

I don't understand these women. They are strong, assertive, intelligent women, why do they need permission to dance?

Jillian's brows rise.

Leo's cocks.

Finally, she rolls her eyes and says, "May I?"

"May you what?" Leo asks, his arm relaxed on the back of

the chair.

She puts her hands on her hips. "May I dance with Layla?"

"Yes. Since you asked so pretty."

She beams at him.

He gives her a once over. "But before you do, since you girls are giving everyone a heart attack, you need something a little more overt to show you're not available."

Apparently, in this crowd an engagement ring isn't enough. I swallow hard. Feeling lost and small. I want to be back in my world where I feel like I matter. Tonight, I feel invisible.

Jillian's expression fills with excitement. "Yes."

He points to the floor at his feet. "Kneel."

She drops like a stone.

I hold my breath.

Michael chimes in, "I really don't want to see this."

"Too bad." Leo shifts, pulling out something black from his back pocket.

He doesn't say anything else.

I blink. It's… a dog collar.

Or at least, that's what it looks like.

Jillian appears about to hyperventilate.

Leo cups her chin and raises her face to his. "Who do you belong to?"

"You." There is complete adoration on her face.

"That's right." He leans down and kisses her lips, and their mouths don't seem to touch as much as cling to each other. "You're mine."

"Yes." She breathes the word like a whisper that floats over my skin.

Have I ever belonged? Anywhere? To anyone? I blink back the sudden sting in my eyes.

He kisses her again. "I love you, Jillian."

"I love you too."

He straightens and slips the thin, black leather around her neck. He clasps it at her nape, and then runs his fingers between her skin and the band. She shivers.

When he shifts in his chair I see there's a silver circle at the center. He hooks his index finger into it and tugs before whispering something I can't hear in her ear.

She closes her eyes as she listens to him.

The words slip into my mind, unbidden. Uninvited. Unwelcome.

I want that.

I look away.

And catch Chad watching me with a peculiar expression on his face. Watchful. Thoughtful.

I don't like it. I feel like he's caught me, like I've revealed something to him. I drop my gaze to stare into my glass. I don't want to witness any more of what I feel is a private moment. But the picture they make is too compelling and I can't help but turn my gaze back to them.

Leo strokes her cheek. "You go have fun."

"I will."

He kisses her again, deep and soulful, and when he lifts his head, he takes her hand and says, "Up you go."

Jillian stands and grins at Layla. "You ready?"

"I am." Layla turns to me. "Come on, let's go."

I shake my head, not trusting my own voice. The last thing I can do is dance.

Layla holds her hands in a prayer. "Pretty please."

I pick up my drink and shake it, shoving my emotions down where they belong. "Give me a minute, then I'll join you."

Michael slips a hand on Layla's thigh and squeezes. "I'll make sure she doesn't fall into any evil clutches."

As if. I'd think I was a ghost if people weren't talking to me.

Layla doesn't take her gaze off me and I can tell by her expression she's concerned. "Promise?"

"Promise." It's a lie. But there are a thousand promises she broke to me when she was in the worst of her depression; I feel I'm owed this tiny one.

Her brow furrows, but then she hooks her arm in Jillian's and off they go.

Michael turns to Leo, his expression pained. "At least you take good care of her."

"Always." Leo raises his glass and they toast.

"Just make sure I'm far away when you... do whatever it is you're going to do."

Leo nods. "I'll wait until you're upstairs. But you'll need to give me at least an hour."

"Done," Michael says.

An hour? What could possibly take an hour?

Brandon slips into an empty chair and juts his chin in their direction. "Even marked they'll have to beat the boys away with a stick."

Michael and Leo don't look too worried.

Suddenly, Brandon glances in my direction. "And what about you, girl?"

My stomach drops. "What about me?"

He smirks. "Are you interested in trying anything out?"

I shake my head vehemently, trying in vein to will the flush spreading over my skin to cool.

He laughs. "When they're busy, how about I at least give you a tour?"

I don't want to contemplate being alone, but I don't want to be an obligation either. I clear my throat. "Oh, well, thanks, but I know you've got a lot going on tonight, and I don't want to be an imposition."

"Not at all. It will be my pleasure."

"I couldn't."

He pins me with a hard-eyed stare. "I insist."

Any additional protests die on my lips. "All right."

"It's settled then." He gives Chad a look. "You can come too, but Mandy has her eye on you, and she can be very persuasive."

Chad shrugs. "We'll see."

The girl in question comes up and passes out drinks. She gives Chad a doe-eyed look and runs a hand down his arm. "Do you require anything else, sir?"

Chad grins at her. He looks boyish and not at all menacing.

"What did you have in mind?"

Mandy bats her lashes. "I'd love to give you a personal tour."

He raises a brow. "Any place in particular?"

I find I have a sudden urge to scream at her that I'm right here. But why? Maybe I'm perturbed at her presumption that he couldn't possibly be with me.

She lowers her head in a demure fashion that seems feigned, not at all like the feeling I get from Jillian and Layla. "Wouldn't you rather be surprised?"

"Let's play it by ear." His expression is affable and charming, but I don't want to think too much about the relief I feel at his noncommittal answer.

She flashes him a brilliant smile. "I promise I'll be very good."

"Isn't it time for you to get back to work, Mandy?" Brandon points to the group off to our left. There's a man on the floor on all fours, naked except for a pair of tiny shorts and a woman that has her high-heeled boots digging into his back. I wince.

That has to hurt.

Mandy's spine snaps ruler straight. "Yes, sir."

She walks away.

I grind my teeth and hide my clenched hands under the table.

I don't want to look in Chad's direction, but I find I'm unable to help myself. Somehow I'm not surprised to find his gaze on me. His eyes are blue. The crystal-clear blue of summer skies. He's intent, direct and unflinching.

Something that feels suspiciously like tension thickens the air between us.

I want to look away. Need to look away.

But I find I can't.

"Jesus Christ," Michael says, breaking the hold Chad has on me.

I jerk my attention away and nearly choke when I spot Layla and Jillian dancing together.

Leo laughs. "You can't say Layla doesn't have an interesting sense of humor."

Michael mutters something under his breath and rakes his hand through his hair. "She is going to pay for this."

I suck in my breath a little shocked.

Jillian and Layla are dancing, their bodies close, their hips an erotic sway in time with each other. They look like sex.

Brandon grins. "For our sakes, I certainly hope you're not going to break them up soon."

"Shut up, Brandon," Michael says.

Leo shrugs. "You won't get an argument from me."

Their hips brush together.

Their arms draped around each other.

Their breasts touch, then part, then touch again.

I heat and flush, and even though I'm not partial to women, they make such a gorgeous sight it's hard not to become hypnotized by their slow, sensual dance.

They are clearly putting on a show, smiling at each other, flirting.

There's a crowd starting to gather around them.

The thin strap of Layla's dress slips off her shoulder and down her arm, dipping the fabric of her dress perilously low.

Leo kicks back in his chair and watches. "My girl does like to put herself on display, and I hate to deny her."

Layla's top slips down, flashing her breast before she raises her hands above her head and the fabric falls back into place. Jillian runs her hands down Layla's waist.

Someone whistles.

The crowd seems to press in on them.

It's sexy. And erotic.

I'm straight and in that moment I want them. Want to be them. Want to fall into that special place they seem to go where they forget everything.

I know why they are doing it.

They want to be seen.

They want their men to see them.

They want to be taken in hand.

A secret part of me longs for that feeling, that magic I seem to be missing.

The music grows and crests, matching the pounding rhythm of my heartbeat.

For a moment, just a moment, I allow myself to imagine being there with them, stirring lust in the hearts of others, making people want me. Losing myself in the music.

My breath quickens.

I'm captivated.

The song ends, and that suspension in time evaporates into the ether.

Michael and Leo both crook their fingers.

And I'm left cold. Ruby

I sit at the table as the three guys talk around me, all apparently in a hell of a good mood.

The only person not having a good time is me.

I'm still reeling from Chad's revelation. I mean, how can that be? Him of all people? Leo and Michael I get—they have a way about them—but Chad is just an affable, good guy.

How did I end up the only straight-laced person here?

"Ruby?" A male voice rips me from my thoughts.

I blink, finding Michael, Leo and Chad staring at me. I've missed something. I frown. "Sorry?"

Chad points at the waitress, a pretty brunette dressed as an angel in all white. "Do you want something to drink?"

I wish I had someone monitoring my drinks. I blink again. Where did that come from? I want no such thing. I don't want anyone telling me what to do. Ever.

So why did that thought pop into my head? It must be the care in the act. Because I can't remember the last guy that even opened the door for me.

That must be it.

It's the care, not the intent.

In a flash of memory, I see my dad, sitting at the table reading his paper, while my mom bustled around him like a happy, little homemaker. It had made me ill. She could have

56

been so much more. Once she'd been a promising violinist, but she'd abandoned all that for my dad.

She'd given up her dreams. Her goals. Her life. So she could do his bidding.

I was not that kind of girl.

"Ruby?" Chad says again. "She's waiting."

The girl flutters her lashes at him and gives him a coy, flirty look.

Something thuds in my chest. Something I don't like and refuse to name.

I clear my throat. "Vodka soda, please."

"Coming right up." The angel girl bites her lip and looks at Chad. "My break's in a couple hours."

Chad grins at her. "I'm sure you'll find me if you need something."

"Oh, I will." Her tone so full of seduction I have a sudden urge to punch her.

How does she know he's not my date? That I'm not a contender?

She gives him a hungry once over before turning with a swish of her hips, sashaying off with an exaggerated sway for Chad's benefit.

That knot sits in my stomach and I pick up a napkin and twist it. I shouldn't have come. I'm not in the right frame of mind. Instead of something fun and interesting that will appease my curiosity, I'm suffering from a mess of emotions that confuse me.

Maybe I should make up an excuse and go home.

But I can't do that, Layla will insist on following me and I can't ruin her night. I know how much she's looking forward to this.

I'll slip away when she goes to the private room Brandon arranged for Michael and Layla.

With an escape planned, the tension in my shoulders eases and I blow out a slow breath.

Leo raises a brow at Chad. "She looks promising."

Chad shrugs, but doesn't say anything.

"You can ask Brandon what she's into, he'll know," Leo says.

Chad turns his gaze to where the waitress is leaning over the bar, working at the computer. "If I'm interested, I'll find out myself."

That queasiness settles in my throat.

I'm not jealous.

I mean, why would I be jealous? I'm not attracted to Chad. But I find that I'm… well, I don't know what I am. I just had it in my head he'd be the odd man out with me. That while the couples went off and did their kinky things, we'd sit in the corner, drink and have a good laugh at all this nonsense. But it turns out, with the dark-haired bombshell waitress, I could end up sitting here alone.

The notion makes me even more determined to slip out the second Layla and Michael go off for their private escapade.

And speak of the devil.

Layla and Jillian emerge from the crowd now littering the floor, swaying to the music thumping loud over the speakers.

They look exactly right. Exactly like they belong.

Like sex and sin.

Heaven and hell.

People part for them; men stop what they are doing and stare after them, a look of stunned awe on their faces.

I swallow hard.

Michael shakes his head. "That's trouble."

"Agreed," Leo says, his voice amused, but his dark eyes are on Jillian. Hot and possessive.

"What's it going to be? Should we get them in line now? Or later." Michael scrubs a hand over his jaw.

"Later. Let's see what kind of rope they hang themselves with," Leo says.

Michael nods. "Agreed."

A man tries to stop Layla, his hand encircling her wrist. She shakes her head and points to the necklace around her throat, a fine, delicate silver chain with a lock and key hanging off it. After all this time the significance of the charm finally registers in my brain. It's a symbol of ownership. The man nods, and promptly removes his hands.

He gives Jillian the eye, but she flashes her engagement ring, before pointing at the table. At Leo.

The man looks over at us, grins, and raises his glass in a toast.

Leo chuckles. "I almost feel sorry for him." He crooks his finger at Jillian. "Almost."

Layla and Jillian continue their slow strut across the room, their hips a provocative sway, their breasts thrust out.

Brandon comes up to the table, props himself up against the couch, and whistles. "Good luck with that."

Michael and Leo grin at each other.

Layla and Jillian stop in front of their men and plop their evening bags on the table. Layla licks her lips, a sly expression on her face. She's slicked her mouth with some sort of crimson gloss. She tilts her head toward the dance floor. "Jillian and I want to dance."

Michael's gaze cruises over her body. "Are you going to be a good girl?"

"Of course."

He nods. "All right then."

Now it's Jillian's turn and she looks at Leo, the question in her eyes.

He looks right back, saying nothing.

I don't understand these women. They are strong, assertive, intelligent women, why do they need permission to dance?

Jillian's brows rise.

Leo's cocks.

Finally, she rolls her eyes and says, "May I?"

"May you what?" Leo asks, his arm relaxed on the back of the chair.

She puts her hands on her hips. "May I dance with Layla?"

"Yes. Since you asked so pretty."

She beams at him.

He gives her a once over. "But before you do, since you girls are giving everyone a heart attack, you need something a little more overt to show you're not available."

Apparently, in this crowd an engagement ring isn't enough. I swallow hard. Feeling lost and small. I want to be back in my world where I feel like I matter. Tonight, I feel invisible.

Jillian's expression fills with excitement. "Yes."

He points to the floor at his feet. "Kneel."

She drops like a stone.

I hold my breath.

Michael chimes in, "I really don't want to see this."

"Too bad." Leo shifts, pulling out something black from his back pocket.

He doesn't say anything else.

I blink. It's… a dog collar.

Or at least, that's what it looks like.

Jillian appears about to hyperventilate.

Leo cups her chin and raises her face to his. "Who do you belong to?"

"You." There is complete adoration on her face.

"That's right." He leans down and kisses her lips, and their mouths don't seem to touch as much as cling to each other. "You're mine."

"Yes." She breathes the word like a whisper that floats over my skin.

Have I ever belonged? Anywhere? To anyone? I blink back the sudden sting in my eyes.

He kisses her again. "I love you, Jillian."

"I love you too."

He straightens and slips the thin, black leather around her neck. He clasps it at her nape, and then runs his fingers between her skin and the band. She shivers.

When he shifts in his chair I see there's a silver circle at the center. He hooks his index finger into it and tugs before whispering something I can't hear in her ear.

She closes her eyes as she listens to him.

The words slip into my mind, unbidden. Uninvited. Unwelcome.

I want that.

I look away.

And catch Chad watching me with a peculiar expression on his face. Watchful. Thoughtful.

I don't like it. I feel like he's caught me, like I've revealed something to him. I drop my gaze to stare into my glass. I don't want to witness any more of what I feel is a private moment. But the picture they make is too compelling and I can't help but turn my gaze back to them.

Leo strokes her cheek. "You go have fun."

"I will."

He kisses her again, deep and soulful, and when he lifts his head, he takes her hand and says, "Up you go."

Jillian stands and grins at Layla. "You ready?"

"I am." Layla turns to me. "Come on, let's go."

I shake my head, not trusting my own voice. The last thing I can do is dance.

Layla holds her hands in a prayer. "Pretty please."

I pick up my drink and shake it, shoving my emotions down where they belong. "Give me a minute, then I'll join you."

Michael slips a hand on Layla's thigh and squeezes. "I'll make sure she doesn't fall into any evil clutches."

As if. I'd think I was a ghost if people weren't talking to me.

Layla doesn't take her gaze off me and I can tell by her expression she's concerned. "Promise?"

"Promise." It's a lie. But there are a thousand promises she broke to me when she was in the worst of her depression; I feel I'm owed this tiny one.

Her brow furrows, but then she hooks her arm in Jillian's and off they go.

Michael turns to Leo, his expression pained. "At least you take good care of her."

"Always." Leo raises his glass and they toast.

"Just make sure I'm far away when you... do whatever it is you're going to do."

Leo nods. "I'll wait until you're upstairs. But you'll need to give me at least an hour."

"Done," Michael says.

An hour? What could possibly take an hour?

Brandon slips into an empty chair and juts his chin in their direction. "Even marked they'll have to beat the boys away with a stick."

Michael and Leo don't look too worried.

Suddenly, Brandon glances in my direction. "And what about you, girl?"

My stomach drops. "What about me?"

He smirks. "Are you interested in trying anything out?"

I shake my head vehemently, trying in vein to will the flush spreading over my skin to cool.

He laughs. "When they're busy, how about I at least give you a tour?"

I don't want to contemplate being alone, but I don't want to be an obligation either. I clear my throat. "Oh, well, thanks, but I know you've got a lot going on tonight, and I don't want to be an imposition."

"Not at all. It will be my pleasure."

"I couldn't."

He pins me with a hard-eyed stare. "I insist."

Any additional protests die on my lips. "All right."

"It's settled then." He gives Chad a look. "You can come too, but Mandy has her eye on you, and she can be very persuasive."

Chad shrugs. "We'll see."

The girl in question comes up and passes out drinks. She gives Chad a doe-eyed look and runs a hand down his arm. "Do you require anything else, sir?"

Chad grins at her. He looks boyish and not at all menacing. "What did you have in mind?"

Mandy bats her lashes. "I'd love to give you a personal tour."

He raises a brow. "Any place in particular?"

I find I have a sudden urge to scream at her that I'm right here. But why? Maybe I'm perturbed at her presumption that he couldn't possibly be with me.

She lowers her head in a demure fashion that seems feigned, not at all like the feeling I get from Jillian and Layla. "Wouldn't you rather be surprised?"

"Let's play it by ear." His expression is affable and charming, but I don't want to think too much about the relief I feel at his noncommittal answer.

She flashes him a brilliant smile. "I promise I'll be very good."

"Isn't it time for you to get back to work, Mandy?" Brandon points to the group off to our left. There's a man on the floor on all fours, naked except for a pair of tiny shorts and a woman that has her high-heeled boots digging into his back. I wince.

That has to hurt.

Mandy's spine snaps ruler straight. "Yes, sir."

She walks away.

I grind my teeth and hide my clenched hands under the table.

I don't want to look in Chad's direction, but I find I'm unable to help myself. Somehow I'm not surprised to find his gaze on me. His eyes are blue. The crystal-clear blue of summer skies. He's intent, direct and unflinching.

Something that feels suspiciously like tension thickens the air between us.

I want to look away. Need to look away.

But I find I can't.

"Jesus Christ," Michael says, breaking the hold Chad has on me.

I jerk my attention away and nearly choke when I spot Layla and Jillian dancing together.

Leo laughs. "You can't say Layla doesn't have an interesting sense of humor."

Michael mutters something under his breath and rakes his hand through his hair. "She is going to pay for this."

I suck in my breath a little shocked.

Jillian and Layla are dancing, their bodies close, their hips an erotic sway in time with each other. They look like sex.

Brandon grins. "For our sakes, I certainly hope you're not going to break them up soon."

"Shut up, Brandon," Michael says.

Leo shrugs. "You won't get an argument from me."

Their hips brush together.

Their arms draped around each other.

Their breasts touch, then part, then touch again.

I heat and flush, and even though I'm not partial to women, they make such a gorgeous sight it's hard not to become hypnotized by their slow, sensual dance.

They are clearly putting on a show, smiling at each other, flirting.

There's a crowd starting to gather around them.

The thin strap of Layla's dress slips off her shoulder and down her arm, dipping the fabric of her dress perilously low.

Leo kicks back in his chair and watches. "My girl does like to put herself on display, and I hate to deny her."

Layla's top slips down, flashing her breast before she raises her hands above her head and the fabric falls back into place. Jillian runs her hands down Layla's waist.

Someone whistles.

The crowd seems to press in on them.

It's sexy. And erotic.

I'm straight and in that moment I want them. Want to be them. Want to fall into that special place they seem to go where they forget everything.

I know why they are doing it.

They want to be seen.

They want their men to see them.

They want to be taken in hand.

A secret part of me longs for that feeling, that magic I seem to be missing.

The music grows and crests, matching the pounding rhythm of my heartbeat.

For a moment, just a moment, I allow myself to imagine being there with them, stirring lust in the hearts of others, making people want me. Losing myself in the music.

My breath quickens.

I'm captivated.

The song ends, and that suspension in time evaporates into the ether.

Michael and Leo both crook their fingers.

And I'm left cold.

8.

Layla

I'm breathing hard. I look at Jillian and wink. "I think we caught their attention."

"I'd say so." Jillian grins, smoothing her hand over her red dress. "Along with half the place."

Leo and Michael crook their fingers in perfect synchronicity, beckoning us to them.

I take a deep breath. "We're going to have to pay now."

"I hope it's worth it," Jillian says.

I really don't know what Michael will do to me, but I'm not naive. I'm wanting something. I'm not the exhibitionist Jillian is, but I do like a good public claiming. Usually Michael and I play our public games privately, in the corner booth at restaurants, slipping off unseen at parties only to return, my hair a bit too messy, my lips a bit too full. But tonight isn't for that.

The whole purpose of this kind of party, this kind of night, is to be seen. And I want other men to want me. To wish they were Michael.

"You ready?" Jillian asks.

"I am."

We walk together, and the crowd parts for us as we stride toward our men, waiting for us with dark, commanding expressions on their faces.

I'm almost hyperventilating by the time I'm standing in front of Michael. When I stop I give him a little wave and say in a breathless voice, "Hi."

He gives me a wry smile. "Having fun, sugar?"

"Yes." I tilt my head toward Jillian. "Your sister is a good dancer."

He crosses his arms. "Are you looking for a girl to fuck?"

"No." I straighten and give him a smile. "We were dancing."

He knows I don't have any interest in girls. I don't have any interest in anyone but him. I wanted to tease him. For fun.

He's playing a good game, but he understands this. There was a time when I'd forgotten how to tease, how to have fun, how to live. I'd been a shell going through the motions of life, living like a ghost.

He'd changed all that for me.

Every day I test a little more, expand my boundaries and my limits. I remember who I am and who I want to be.

He cocks a brow. "So you decided to put on a show with my sister, is that it?"

I bite my lower lip, trying to look innocent. "Maybe it was a little twisted."

"Not from where I stood, darling girl," Brandon says helpfully.

I beam at him. "Thank you."

"Don't pull that innocent act with me." Michael's tone is no-nonsense. He means business.

I try not to melt into the floor.

"And what do you have to say for yourself?" Leo asks Jillian.

"We were just having a little fun," Jillian says, batting her lashes at him.

"At your brother's expense?" Leo asks.

Jillian presses her lips together and I know she's trying not to giggle. "That's what little sisters are for."

Leo laughs and shakes his head.

Michael scowls, but his lips quirk in what I know is amusement. "You're lucky she's my sister, or you'd be making good on what you were doling out. But you're safe from that with her here. So we'll need to take this private."

I don't say anything. From a wealth of experience, talking will just make matters worse.

Michael tilts his head and gives me a speculative once over. He cocks a brow at Brandon. "Is that room ready?"

"It is," Brandon says, but I don't even glance at him.

I gulp. It's time. Nerves race through me. Followed quickly by excitement that slicks my thighs.

I want this so bad. For him to take me this way. It's not that I'm even into bondage. It's just that I want to reclaim the horrible night that changed the course of my life forever. I want to obliterate its power over me.

More important, I don't want Michael to have to be careful with me anymore. I don't want him to have to worry about triggering a panic attack if he gets too forceful, I don't want him to have to hold back for me.

As much as he's empowered me, I want to empower him in return.

Maybe it's too much to ask, I don't know. But I want to find out.

"Are you ready?" Michael stands and looks down at me. I remember the first time I looked up at him, he seemed to go on and on, and his shoulders had blocked out everyone in that club but him. Even back then, when he'd terrified me, I'd known he was safe.

Known he was meant for me.

Unlike that first night, I take his hand, and raise my lips to his. "I am."

9.

Jillian

As I watch my brother and Layla follow Brandon, I experience a sudden tremble of nerves. It was all fun and games when Michael was here and I was protected from Leo's plans. It's not so much that I want protection, because I want to be pushed tonight, but this is something new. Something unfamiliar.

Leo will test my boundaries, and his own.

Michael and Layla's presence delayed the inevitable and gave me free rein to indulge my most depraved fantasies without having to contemplate too much of the reality.

Leo stands, looks me up and down, and sighs. "What to do with wayward girls?"

I give him my most playful smile. "I'm sure you have some ideas."

"I do." He glances behind him and says, "You'd better move your drinks."

I gulp as Ruby and Chad swipe their glasses off the table

with alarming speed.

Leo steps aside and points. "Get on the table, Jillian."

I stare at the surface in terrified horror, my nerves getting the better of me. In the year we've been together, Leo has pushed my exhibitionist buttons many, many times but they have always been safe. We have an agreement that nobody will ever touch me—because neither of us wants that. It's a hard limit as they say—but he's still determined to fulfill these little twists of mine.

He's let Brandon watch me in the privacy of our own home.

He's taken pictures of me.

Fucked me in places where we risked getting caught. Taken me in public, tucked away in some dark corner, his hand over my mouth to quell my screams as not to interrupt the strangers not far away.

I've loved it all. Especially since he's always there, protecting me, guiding me. I shiver. Watching me.

And, I can't deny my rather telling fantasies of being forced on display, as he well knows. But now that reality is upon me, I'm suddenly not sure I'm ready to come face-to-face with my desires.

I freeze in my spot, staring at the table as though it might reach out and grab me.

"Now." Leo's tone is a bark propelling me into action.

I climb on and meet Ruby's wide, stunned eyes. *Right there with ya, sweet cheeks. I can't believe this either.*

"Facing me," Leo says.

I swivel until I face him, kneel and blink up at him.

There's already a crowd starting to gather, both men and women. All dressed in black, white, pink or red in honor of the Valentine's theme, all watching me with intent, interested gazes. My stomach jumps, heats. I gulp.

I shift my attention to Leo, my anchor. I lick my lips. "Leo?"

He strokes a finger down my cheek and lowers his head until his lips touch the shell of my ear and whispers, "Haven't you been wanting something just like this?"

My throat tightens, but I manage to squeak out. "But. You?"

I can't help thinking of that time, not so long ago, where Leo pushed himself past his own limits trying to give me something he thought I wanted and how it almost ended us. Not that I have that worry now, because we are stronger than ever, and our bond is unbreakable. We made a promise to each other that night he sang under my window to always communicate and we've kept our promise.

But I'm still scared. Scared it doesn't excite him as much as it excites me. I know how he is, how much he wants to give me what he thinks I need, even at the expense of his own comfort.

I don't want him to do something he doesn't want.

It's not worth it.

He brushes his mouth over mine and strokes a finger over my cheek. "Trust me."

"I do," I say, because I trust him to do right by me. I just don't trust him to do right by himself. I wind my arms around his neck and pull him close, so nobody can overhear what we're saying. "But all I need, is you. I don't need this to be happy. I'm already happy."

He squeezes me tight and whispers back, "I know you are, Jilly. You've been working so hard at school and you've been such a good girl. I want you to have this."

When I start to protest, he takes my hand and presses my open palm to his hard cock. "Does it feel like I don't want this?"

I curl my hand over his erection. "No."

"Trust me." He takes my hand and puts it around my back. "We have one hour and the only reason I'm allowing this is because it's a closed, private party with limited people. So enjoy it now. You may not get the opportunity again."

My lashes flutter open and I take in the gathering crowd behind me, some of them I know from other events, some of them I don't. But if Brandon has them here, I know they are safe. Leo is giving this to me, it's his present, and he sounds sure. It's only right to surrender to his will. I nod. "Okay."

His teeth scrape over the line of my jaw. "Give them a show. Make them want you."

Then he stands back, and assesses me like I'm up for auction. All my trepidation fades away and a new type of nervousness takes its place. Filled with anticipation and excitement. Before Leo, I never understood how that was possible, to be simultaneously scared and turned on, but I've learned it's a powerful cocktail.

He taps my legs. "Open."

I comply. While my dress looks like pure latex, the skirt is pleated and loose, made from a stretchy material that allows maximum give.

Leo gives me a hard-eyed stare that makes me shiver with lust. He looks at my splayed thighs. "More."

My legs open obscenely wide and I can feel the air brush against my wet, slick, wanting folds. I can already feel the beginning of that special place I go to where I no longer fight. That switch being flipped in my head that makes me up for anything.

It's when the Jillian I am to the outside world slips away, and the Jillian that belongs only to Leo takes her place.

He's still not satisfied. He grips my thighs and presses them farther apart until my muscles strain. I suck in my breath as my dress slides indecently up my legs, the fabric bunching at my hips.

I gulp. This is happening. This is real. It's not a dream I'm talking about and exploring on my couch while Leo plays over my clit, but real.

Behind him, I see people stopping to watch, enjoying the show.

My body clenches.

Leo smiles, and then turns to a guy standing next to him. "What do you think?"

The guy is handsome, blond and tall, dressed in a business suit. He steps closer to me, close enough to see the gold shards in his brown eyes.

"No touching," Leo says.

The guy nods, puts his hands behind his back and starts to circle me.

I glance at Leo and his dark eyes are hot and hungry on mine, he nods.

I shiver, my brain caught in a suspended place between living my fantasy and uncertainty.

The guy comes to stand in front of me again. I give him a brilliant smile and he chuckles. "Having fun, girl?"

Am I? I lick my lips. "Yes."

He shifts his attention to Leo. "She's quite beautiful. But it seems like she's missing something."

"I agree," Leo says and steps back up. "I know just the thing."

Right in front of the stranger, he slides his fingers deep inside me, and I gasp at the sudden, forceful shock of his entry. When he pulls away, his fingers are slick with my wetness. He paints my lips with the evidence of my desire, the undeniable proof that I'm exactly this kind of girl. He does it again, his thumb on my clit. I pulse in his hand on a stuttery gasp.

He retreats, and once again paints my lips so my arousal fills my senses, making me feel like everyone in this room is experiencing it right along with me. It only heightens the exposure. Fuels my desire.

Leo once again steps back. "She's still missing something."

And suddenly, Brandon is next to him, looking me up and down. He shrugs. "She's not very exposed, now is she?"

"Good point," Leo says, as though he's given the matter serious thought.

I wrinkle my nose at Brandon, who grins at me, steps up and whispers in my ear, "You don't fool me, I know who you are."

They don't fool me either. I know how they operate. Leo knows exactly what he's going to do, and how. He doesn't leave important things like this to chance.

With Brandon standing in front of me, Leo comes to stand

next to him. "This isn't going to work at all."

"Nope." Brandon crosses his arms.

"If you're going to be a cock tease, you might as well go all the way and do it properly, don't you think?" Leo asks, his head tilted.

I don't say anything. I'm not sure I can speak. I might hyperventilate.

Brandon smiles at me. "In the back, I have a room set up just for her. All it has is a table and a spotlight."

Leo cocks a brow. "Sounds right up your alley, doesn't it?"

I can only gulp. Is he really going to do this? Allow strangers to watch as he takes me? Do I want that?

Leo slides his fingers up my thighs, and he's hitting slick flesh before he even reaches any place good. "Someone likes that idea."

If I'm so aroused, I must, right?

"Why am I not surprised?" Brandon asks.

Leo hooks his fingers into the silver circle at my throat. "You're mine. And you're going to show every single person here that you perform for me. Understand?"

I'm going to combust. Right here at the table. In front of god and everyone. "Yes, Leo."

He tugs and the leather band around my throat tightens. "Let's go."

And down the rabbit's hole I go.

10.

Ruby

Leo and Jillian walk away and I sit there, drink in hand, staring into the clear bubbly liquid. My heart is pounding hard, and my cheeks feel hot. I want to press the cool glass against my forehead to soothe my flushed skin.

"You okay there?" Chad asks, his voice thoughtful.

I jerk my attention to him, blinking back to the reality of my surroundings, surprised to find I'm in what now looks like a very upscale, expensive club. I clear my throat. "Yep, I'm good."

"Are you sure?" Chad's blue eyes peer into me, expression intent on my face.

I swallow and nod. "Yes." But my voice doesn't sound at all sure.

He smiles and slides his glass down on the table before taking my own from my fingers and placing it next to his. "It's okay to be overwhelmed, you know. It's normal."

I want to object that I'm perfectly fine, but something stops me. Maybe it's the set of his jaw. The way he's looking at me, not with judgment or arrogance, but with what looks like genuine concern. I find myself asking, "It is?"

He nods then chuckles. "The first time I went to this kind of party I was in shock. It was like a train wreck where I couldn't look away."

My eyes widen and some of the tension knotting my stomach eases. "Yes, that's exactly what it feels like."

"You're not alone, I think it's like that for everyone." He rubs his hand along the back of his neck and laughs. "The first time I went with a friend of mine, and I wasn't into the scene at all. He took me to a hardcore leather club. My first and last trip."

"You didn't like it?"

He shudders before flashing me a grin. "I walked in, and it was dark. Like a cave. The first scene I passed was a woman sewing a guy's lips together. I almost passed out from the shock."

I cringe. "Oh my god, I'd have died."

"I almost did." He winces. "I've never been into that kind of extreme pain, needles and instruments." He shivers. "I hate blood. Much to my father's disappointment."

"Why would your dad be disappointed?" It's hard to imagine him being a disappointment to anyone.

He shrugs. "I come from a family of doctors. Being a computer geek is kind of a letdown."

It's something we have in common and it surprises me. "I can understand that. My family thinks I'm from outer space. Although, you'd be right up their alley."

He grins. "Why's that?"

I shrug and wave my hand over him. "You're all clean cut and employed."

He laughs. "That's all it takes, huh?"

"They have simple requirements." Whatever he's doing is working, because I'm starting to relax. That horrible lonely feeling is starting to fade. I want to kiss him in gratitude. "So, if you weren't into that scene, why did you go?"

He tilts his head. "Same reason as you, I was curious."

I bite my lower lip and he tracks the movement. I contemplate, but find myself admitting the truth to him. "I wish I'd stayed home."

He drains his glass and shifts to face me more fully, putting his arm on the back of the couch where we're sitting. "Why didn't you?"

I blow out a breath and shrug. "I guess I wanted to see what the fuss was about."

"And do you? See the fuss?"

Do I? I shake my head. "I don't think I get it."

He nods, but doesn't ask me more questions.

"Aren't you going to try and convince me I'm wrong?" I'm not sure why I ask, maybe because everyone seems so sure this is better.

His eyes narrow on me. "Nope."

I experience a stirring of awareness, not sexual, just… something. "Why?"

"If it doesn't turn you on, it doesn't turn you on." Over my head, he catches the attention of someone in back of me, raises his hand and signals for two more drinks. "It's not up to me to decide that for you."

I drain my glass and stare into the ice cubes, glittering under the soft light. "It's hard, you know, when they all seem so in love."

"Yeah, I can see that." He laughs. "Sometimes they are a bit sickening in their devotion."

He understands. He's listening. I can talk to him and I don't feel like he's judging me. It's a strange experience, this notion I can admit stuff to him I can't admit to my best friend. I clear my throat. "I'm jealous."

"I know. I can see it on your face." He puts his hand on the back of my neck, and his fingers are cool on my overheated skin. I meet his gaze.

As strange as it sounds, I get lost in the blue of his eyes. The soft understanding in them. "You don't think I'm terrible?"

He shakes his head. "I think you're human." His thumb traces down the curve of my throat and tingles break along my skin. "Just remember, Ruby. It's not the kink that makes them that way. It's being with the right person."

I nod, and as he stares into my face, some of my jagged emotions smooth over. I breathe in and out, slow and deep, and an almost meditative haze creeps over me.

He doesn't break eye contact.

Doesn't flinch away.

He just breathes in a rhythm that matches my own until I feel almost calm.

The serenity is ripped away by a female voice. "Anything else?"

Both Chad and mine's head whips to the sound and I see the angel girl from before staring at us. She doesn't look happy. Chad's hand falls away and he gives her that all American smile of his. "I think we're good here, thanks."

The girl looks from me to Chad, back and forth, until it settles on him. "Can I still show you around?"

Chad tilts his head toward me. "Maybe later, I can't leave her alone."

I start to protest, but his hand clasps my bare knee and squeezes. I about jump out of my skin at the contact.

The girl glances at me before offering an overly bright smile. "Maybe later then?"

He nods. "I'll try and catch up with you."

"Okay." She frowns and walks away.

I point after her. "You didn't have to do that."

"I wanted to," Chad says.

"You don't have to babysit me." I don't want him to stay because he's obligated. Because he doesn't want to leave me alone.

He turns and looks at me, his expression taking on that hard edge I've seen Leo, Brandon and Michael wear, reminding me what he is. "If I wanted her, I'd have her."

He doesn't seem inclined to elaborate. I try not to think about my relief at his words. I clear my throat and ask before I can think, "You don't want her? She's beautiful."

"She is." He shrugs and takes a drink. "But I can find a girl like her whenever I want. Don't worry, by the end of the night she'll be on to someone else."

"How do you know?"

"She likes to play as they call it. As long as she finds someone attractive, agreeable, and willing to give her what she wants, she'll be happy."

I tilt my head. "How can you possibly know that?"

He winks at me. "I'd love to say it's some awesome power where I can read a girl's thoughts, but that would be a lie. I suspected. Brandon confirmed."

When did they even have that conversation? Because, I can't recall them talking. It must have been when I was lost in my own head and not paying attention.

I bite my lower lip, pick up a napkin and twist it in my hand. "But still, wouldn't you rather go have fun than sit here and be bored with me?"

"I don't find you boring." He shifts again so he's looking more fully at me. "And I'm not much for casual play scenes. Honestly, *that's* what bores me."

I don't let on, but I can't pretend I'm not happy to hear that. I find I don't want him going off with some other girl. I don't know why, but it's true.

He gives me a smirk. "Besides, she picked me because she thinks I'm easy going and I'm not in the mood to disabuse her of the notion."

The statement is like a jolt of awareness. Nervous, I run a finger over my glass. "I think you're easy going."

"I am," he says, then grins at me. "Until I'm not."

I shake my head. "I don't even know what that means."

He laughs. "Layla told me you sing at The Whisky."

I blink at the sudden subject change. "Yeah. On Thursday and Saturday nights."

"Can I come watch you sometime?"

The question startles me and I blurt, "Why?"

"I like music. Layla told me you have a lovely voice and I'd like to hear it."

"Sure," I say, the words slow. "I certainly can't stop you."

"True." He meets my gaze again. "But I'd respect your wishes if you didn't want me to."

"I'd like that." To my surprise, I think I would.

"Good." He pauses, as though thinking of something before he continues, "And, Ruby."

"Yes?" My voice is a bit breathless.

"I'm not going to leave you here alone."

I want to laugh it off. Make light of the statement. But something stops me, because his words are a relief. I don't want to be left alone. I want someone by my side, protecting me from the roller coaster of emotions bombarding me tonight. So I say with complete sincerity, "Thank you."

"You're welcome."

"Oh good," Brandon says from next to us, having suddenly appeared, "I'm glad you're both still here. How about that tour?"

Until that moment I hadn't realized how close I sat to Chad and I jerk away, feeling caught or guilty somehow.

Brandon flashes me a grin.

I do feel better now. Chad helped me and I can only be grateful. I turn to him. "What do you say?"

He smiles. "I'm game."

"Great." I slide from my seat.

Brandon hooks his arm into mine.

To my surprise, Chad takes the other arm. I'm flanked by them. My heart does a strange little pitter-patter.

"Ready to explore?" Brandon asks.

I'm as ready as I'll ever be. I nod. "Let's go."

11.

Layla

The door clicks closed, shutting Michael and I into a complete, almost eerie silence.

There's nothing special about the room, except for its opulence. The lights are low and intimate, and like the space downstairs, it casts a warm glow over the room. There's a mahogany bed with four carved posts, an intricate, antiqued armoire, and rich hardwood floors.

Michael puts his hands on my shoulders, pushing my hair to one side, before leaning down to kiss my neck. "Remember, this isn't pass or fail."

I stare at the bed. "I know."

"Any hint of panic—at all—we stop." He runs his hands down my arms.

I nod. Since that night I have suffered from panic attacks. Between therapy, Michael and the support of my family they are much better now, much less frequent, but they still do happen. Sneaking over me out of nowhere and seizing me in their grip.

I have strategies to deal with them, but they are a frightening experience.

I want to believe they won't affect me, but I can't be sure. I gulp as nerves slither over me and I remind myself I'm safe with Michael.

He strokes a thumb over the curve of my throat. "I know how bad you want this, Layla."

I crane my neck to look back at him. "Do you? Want this?"

His unusual hazel eyes that capture me so, narrow. "Not at the expense of your emotional wellbeing."

He's too good to me. I reach up and stroke a path down his jaw. "It won't be. All I want is to be what you deserve."

He comes to stand in front of me, cups my jaw and raises my chin. "You are, regardless of if I ever tie you up."

"I understand… I know you mean it, but…" I struggle to explain, to communicate the depth of my feelings for him.

He strokes over my bottom lip. "What?"

I lower my gaze. "You've done so much for me." I take a harsh breath. "Is it so hard to understand I want to give you something of equal value?"

His expression softens, filling with love. "You face your fears every day for me. You've forced yourself to heal for me. Do you not understand the value in that?"

I hadn't looked at it like that. I rise to my tiptoes and kiss his mouth, those cruel lips that have delivered both heaven and hell. "I am trying."

"Succeeding," he corrects. Then his hands fall away and he steps back. "So we understand each other."

"We do." I lick my lips. "I promise any hint I will tell you, but I want a promise in return."

"What's that, sugar?"

I meet his eyes, unflinching and unwavering of what I want from him. "Don't hold back. Don't be careful. I don't want careful. I want you."

Without a word, he steps back and starts circling me, stalking me like a predator and desire bursts across my skin. He slides his hands down my shoulders, taking the straps along with him, exposing my nipples before skimming up my collar bone to twine his fingers around my neck. "You're my possession. I own you."

The words are a drug—made all the more addictive because I believe them wholeheartedly. "Yes."

He slides his hands down my waist, and palms the curve of my ass, where the marks he left earlier are still sore and tender to the touch. I wince, sucking in my breath against the pain. Then he steps back and nods. "Strip."

It's not hard. I'm wearing practically nothing. I let the straps of my dress fall from my wrists and the fabric pools to my feet. His gaze rakes over me, up and down, over and over. He sighs. "You're so damn gorgeous."

My heart swells.

"Put your hands behind your head and splay your legs."

I comply. Tonight, right here and now, it's not about fighting, it's about surrender. The air is cool between my legs where I'm already hot and ready for his touch.

"Very nice." He moves closer, and runs his hands over my nipples, in a slow circular motion, lulling me into a type of hypnotic complacency.

Just as my lashes are starting to drift closed, he pinches the sensitive buds, hard between his thumbs and forefingers, rolling, tugging until my eyes tear with pain.

My belly clenches and I gasp out a strangled breath.

Sometimes I just want to be hurt, and tonight is one of those times.

He lowers his head, lifting one breast to his lips.

I cry out as his teeth bear down. Oh sweet Jesus.

His fingers slide between my legs where I'm already soaking wet. Already longing for him. He rubs my clit.

My legs start to quiver.

My arms burn with the effort to maintain my position.

I think of that first night, when I'd been so terrified of him. Then he'd slipped his hands between my legs to find me wet. He'd almost pushed me to orgasm without even trying.

Just like that night, he pulls back.

I pant up at him.

I'm already needy. Already crave what only he can give me.

His gaze is full of a hunger that matches my own. "You're a greedy girl."

I am.

He walks over to the armoire behind me, and I hear the rummaging of stuff before he returns to me with a flogger in his hands. "To warm you up."

Before I can even get my bearings, he swings like he's pitching a softball and the leather straps strike between my legs in a harsh blow.

The pleasure and pain rise through me and I groan.

He does it again.

And again.

I scream. The orgasm is barreling in on me. Fast. "Michael."

"Don't you dare come, Layla," he says, his voice hard and unrelenting.

I can't begin to describe how it hurts and feels good all at the same time. Feathery little stings that caress my flesh. Sensations all mixing together in my head and making me ache.

He flicks the strands once more across my clit and I grit my teeth and try and think of anything but the pleasure rolling through me, threatening to overtake me.

Then, thankfully he moves away from where I'm most vulnerable, striking across my thighs and stomach. Over my breasts and nipples, until I'm hot all over and my skin is blushed with pink.

He drops the flogger to the floor and stalks over to me, sweeping me up and claiming my mouth in a hard, brutal kiss.

He devours me.

His tongue and lips and mouth claiming me with such delicious force I can only succumb to his will.

He pulls away, and takes my arms, bringing them down to my sides. His eyes burn into me. "I can't wait to fuck this hot, tight cunt of yours."

My muscles clench in desire.

He moves behind me. "Go to the bed and wait for me."

On wobbly legs I stand by the mattress and wait. My heart pounding. My body ready.

He returns and, fully clothed, he rubs against my bare back. "Are you ready?"

"Yes." I believe I am, until he holds out the leather straps that will tether me to the bed.

My throat goes bone dry. I'm here, at the point of no return.

12.

Jillian

This isn't what I expected.

The room is pitch-black except for the spotlight shining on a table in the center. I'm disorientated, thrust from the bright activity of the main room and into inky darkness that seems to envelop me with every step I take.

I'm not sure I like this. Not sure I'm ready to make this fantasy a reality. I clutch Leo's hand as I stumble.

"Leo." His name is an anxious whisper on my lips.

"I've got you, Jilly." His voice grounds me, but does nothing to abate the anxiety now pinging through me at the speed of lightning. All the giddy, happy desire from just moments ago has evaporated into thin air.

I hear the sound of the door opening and closing. Again and again, but when I look behind me, I can't see anyone. It's just black. Fathomless and scary.

Even Brandon has disappeared.

The only thing illuminated in the room is that table and

bright light, where I will be.

The sound of the door is jarring.

I gulp, my muscles tensing. I want to drag my feet.

How many people are in here? Did everyone from the front room follow? I have no idea. There could be a hundred people in here and I'd never know it.

Leo has taken my fantasies quite seriously. I am more than on display. On that table, I will be the only thing you can see in the room. Everything else is dark.

Fear pricks across my skin and I am suddenly regretting all the times I'd talked about this stupid fantasy of mine. I force myself to take a deep breath, slow and steady. Okay, I'll be fine. Leo is here with me. Nothing will happen to me. And this is what I want. What I've been practically begging for.

Leo leads me to the table, which I now see isn't a normal, everyday table, but one that has metal rings sticking out of it. He helps me up. "Kneel, Jillian."

I can only comply. I swivel around, already hot under the bright light shining down on me. So bright it's like a sunlamp. I start to breathe fast. I look behind him, trying to peer into the distance to see who might be there, but there's nothing but endless black.

Leo runs his hands over my body, pulling my attention back to him where it belongs, where I need it to be.

It centers me. Yes, this is what I need. Him.

He grips my neck, pulling me close.

Then his lips are on mine, sucking me in, hypnotizing me. His mouth is hot and possessive. His tongue claiming.

I instantly calm, getting lost in him like I always do, forgetting everyone and everything but him. This is what this man does to me.

When he finally pulls away I blink at him, a bit dazed.

He smiles at me, and strokes my cheek. "Jesus, I love you."

"I love you too," I say without hesitation.

"Enjoy it." He presses a hard, brutal kiss to my lips. "Give in to it."

I nod. His reminder of the people in this room, their eyes

on me, pulls my attention away from him. I lick my lips and straighten my spine, breathing deep as I look into the blackness.

I imagine a hundred eyes on me.

But instead of working me up like it does when I'm sitting in my living room, it cools my blood. Somehow, between the transition of the front room, where it was fun and flirty and a game, to this room where I'm the only thing visible, it's taken on a tone I'm not sure I'm in love with.

Okay, I need to shake it off. Tap into that place where I lose myself. Leo has always commented that I slip into that space ridiculously easy and all I need to do is find it. Between Leo and there, I'll be okay.

This is just new.

Leo steps away then crouches down, only to bring up a long, metal chain that glints in the light. I stare at it, wide eyed. As he gets to the end, I see a hook. He attaches it onto the silver circle at my neck, and then to the table. Capturing me to this time and place.

The metal thuds against my throat, down between the curves of my breasts. He tugs and all my focus zeros back on him. We stare at each other for several long beats and I get lost in his dark, hungry gaze. He wraps the chain around his hand, pulling me close. He whispers against my lips, "You're mine."

"Yes." My nipples pull into tight peaks, almost too tight, reawakening my desire. And I think I'm going to melt into a puddle on the table as my heartbeat speeds up into an impossible gallop. Yes, more of this.

All I need is to focus on him, the man I love, the man I am going to marry and spend my life with.

Leo surveys his work. "Pretty."

I peer into the darkness, trying to discern shadows, but I can see nothing against the lights.

Leo smirks. "They're watching you, girl. Watching as I chain you to this table. Watching you do whatever I tell you to do. And watching you come because of it."

The words take my attention off him and back on the

nameless, faceless crowd. I take in a deep breath and blow it out. Instead of exciting me the way it normally does, I feel some of my lust cool. I don't understand it. I've wanted this for so long. I've played out this exact scenario. But I can't get lost the way I want to.

I can't figure out why.

Leo presses an open-mouth kiss to my throat, pulling me back to him, before whispering in my ear, "How should I hurt you tonight?"

The image of a belt flashes through my head at lightning speed.

I hate the belt.

I love the belt.

I want it on my skin.

I don't want it.

I can't admit it and squeak out, "Your hand?"

Spankings are easier, especially in front of a crowd, where having Leo's hand on my skin will establish the intimacy I so desperately need.

Leo cups my chin and narrows his eyes. "What was your first thought?"

I don't want to say. I shake my head.

"I'm not asking." His voice turns hard and it makes me wary even while it inflames me.

He has that look in his eyes, the one that warns evasion is not recommended. Once upon a time I would have ignored the warning, but I'm smarter now, more experienced. The consequences are always worse than I can imagine. I swallow past my dry throat and peer into the darkness, wondering how many people are witnessing this private moment between us.

I don't think I want it. To have people watch as Leo hits me with the thick black belt at his waist.

"Jillian," his voice says this is my last warning. If I don't answer now, there will be hell to pay.

I'm confused. But I don't lie. "The belt."

Eyes hard, Leo steps back and puts his hand on the buckle. "This belt?"

I nod.

"Should I strip you naked first?"

No! No! No!

I blink into the darkness. I don't want to be naked in front of them.

I frown. He's worked so hard to set this up for me. He's arranged it with Brandon. He's giving me exactly what I want. My fantasies. And I need to make him proud. He told me to give them a show, to make them want me, but how can I do that when I'm so anxious.

I just need to concentrate.

I shake my head.

He raises a brow. "No?"

I shake my head again. "I…" My gaze darts out to the audience. "I don't want to be naked."

He steps forward, cups my jaw, and looks me dead in the eye. "Is there something you want to say, girl?"

I know what he's doing. He's checking to make sure I don't want to safe word out of the scene.

I have never used my safe word. Never had to. I trust Leo and he instinctively knows how far to push me. A new hope surges, maybe he wants me to use it. Maybe he doesn't want this either.

I search his face, but find no stress there. I know him, all his moods. I can read his expressions. But I sense nothing. No unease. No tightening at the corners of his mouth that tell me he's unsure.

He's really okay with this.

I'm the one in my head. Not him.

I need to let this happen. I was gung-ho about this all night, ready, willing and able. I don't know what's changed; I just need to find that place where I was before.

I gulp. "I'm okay."

"You sure?" Now his expression does crease.

"I'm sure." I clench my hands tightly together and lower my gaze to his belt. "I don't think I want to be naked."

He strokes my hair, kisses me on the top of my head but

says nothing.

Instead, he walks behind me, and pulls the tie of the corset he'd lace me into earlier in the privacy of our bedroom. "Is that so?"

The silken tie comes undone at my waist.

I blink, tears welling in my eyes as I stare out into the crowd of people I can't see. This is not how I thought I'd feel. I feel vulnerable, and distant. I can't lose myself.

I don't want these people here. All the fun from before, the teasing and games, that's all it was, and this doesn't feel like that.

Reality is nothing like my fantasies.

I don't want people watching us have sex.

I don't want people to see me naked.

I don't want people to watch Leo hit me with a belt.

Those things are private. For just Leo and me.

I'm not turned on. I'm cold.

Conflict fills my chest. He's pushed past his own limits to give me this because I wanted it. I can't disappoint him. The people watching, I want them to be in awe of Leo. I want him to get the admiration he deserves, because the man is awesome. I don't want these people to see me use my safe word.

I'll have to find a way to power through.

"Jillian," Leo says, his voice soft now. His hands rest on my shoulders.

I can do this. I twist my hands.

I don't know how, but I will try and deliver a performance in front of these strangers.

The thought fills me with such unease my stomach twists.

I've never faked anything with Leo. Do I want to start now?

I don't know how I can do this with the way I feel.

I can't make anyone want me. I can't put on a show. I don't feel sexy.

I feel lost.

I start to cry and utter that one word that will stop

everything. "Red."

13.

Layla

"Turn around and face me." Michael's deep voice shivers through me.

My eyes feel wide as saucers as I stare at the thick leather cuffs on the bed.

I have a momentary flash of rope tight around my wrists, cutting off my circulation. For a brief second, I'm sucked back into that alley and that cold, awful night when my world was changed forever.

I gasp in a breath, let the panic wash over me, and then blink it away. It fades from my mind like an old-fashioned television set, narrowing down into a pinprick of focus before it goes black.

Then I'm back in the room. With Michael.

His hands rest on my shoulders. "You okay?"

I nod.

"Let me hear the words."

"I'm okay."

He soothes over my bare arms. "Turn around and face me."

I do. Slowly pivoting on my high heels until I see his face. It soothes me. Calms me down.

"Good." He runs a finger down my cheek. "I want you to see my face the whole time, so you can remember who's touching you."

"As though I could ever forget."

He tilts my chin. "Eyes on me, girl."

This was Michael's way, how he kept me present. Focused on him and our future and not the nightmares of the past.

He gently circles my right wrist and peers into my eyes, searching with intent.

My shoulders tighten. He's being careful again, cautious.

I give him a bright smile, hoping to reassure him that I have my nerves under control, and he can let loose on me. Because more than anything that is what I want. It's not bondage, it's the symbol of what it represents. I need to put this to bed once and for all so I can be the woman I want to be. A woman Michael doesn't have to hold back with.

His big fingers squeeze on the fine bones. "I can't decide if I should strap you up by the posts, or lay you down on the bed."

That sounds promising. I lick my lips. The faster we get on with it the faster it will be over.

He kisses me, full on the mouth, his tongue laying claim to me for one fraction of a second before retreating. "Let's start standing, shall we?"

"Whatever you want." As long as he starts.

He puts the cuff on my wrist but doesn't fasten it. "Aren't you a good girl?"

The leather is heavy against my skin. They used a rope that night, cutting off my circulation so my hands went numb. This leather is soft. The pressure on my wrists the only reminder of what they'd done.

It makes me hopeful.

He narrows his hazel eyes and again searches my

expression. I relax my jaw so my growing agitation doesn't show. *Please don't be careful. Take me.*

Apparently satisfied with what he's found in my face, he slowly buckles the strap before testing the hold by rubbing his fingers between my skin and the leather.

He's careful. So damn careful.

This isn't what I want.

I want lust and passion.

I want him to be overwhelmed with the desire to consume me.

I want to be taken as only he can take me.

I want him to fucking devour me.

I blow out an exasperated breath and he raises his head from his work and gives me an arched brow. "Problems?"

Indignation fills my throat and leaves my mouth before I can stop it. "You promised."

His jaw hardens. "Stop trying to control things, Layla."

"But you promised."

His gaze lasers in on me. "Who's in charge here? Me? Or you?"

Okay, I need to calm down. I'm overanxious and letting it get the best of me. "You. But—"

He holds up a hand, cutting me off. "No buts. Just stand there and be quiet."

Words, a million of them, fly through my head, but I press my lips together. Reminding myself this is about surrender. That I trust Michael. That my impatience, my desire to be free from that single event that changed the trajectory of my life, is what's driving this desire to hurry things along.

He goes back to what he was doing, once again testing the straps before moving to the other wrist. He buckles me in with the same methodical care.

I barely pay attention. I stare at his dark, bent head and blurt, "Don't ignore me."

He growls. "You're trying my patience."

"Well good," I snap.

Without a word he shakes his head, and sighs before

returning to the wardrobe and pulling out leather ankle cuffs.

This isn't how I envisioned things.

I pictured romantic and passionate. Pictured him snapping the cuffs in place before kissing me roughly. I need consuming. To get lost in him. So I can forget.

How can I obliterate that night when I'm cold? When he's being clinical, and calculating?

I huff and puff and roll my eyes. He completely ignores me.

Instead, he pulls what looks like short straps from the wardrobe, and walks around me, clipping one end to my wrist and the other to the post.

All the while my anger and agitation grows.

He kneels down and makes quick work of the straps on my ankles. He strikes my thigh somewhere between a tap and a slap, and I spread my legs, glaring down at him.

"Michael."

"Enough, Layla." His words hold that distinct bite, but it doesn't cause the normal shiver of lust. Because that's not dominance in his voice, it's anger.

I hear the ripping of Velcro, a tug on my leg while he tethers me to the post and moves to my other leg.

I don't want to ruin this, and instinct warns me to be quiet, but I can't seem to stop talking. "All I'm trying to say is—"

He squeezes my thigh; hard enough I gasp and lose my train of thought. Then he jerks the straps and everything stretches and tightens.

I still.

He steps back.

I test my mobility and find I can't move.

I'm splayed wide and open, taut. Unable to get away. Unable to run and hide.

I experience a momentary burst of panic. It twists inside me then dissolves.

Michael turns away and walks over to the chair resting against the wall. He picks it up and brings it over in front of me before he sits down.

Resting his arms on the chair, he leans back.

I blink at him. "What are you doing?"

He gives me a hard look. "You're pissing me off and I'm not going to touch you while I'm angry."

I tilt my chin. The tides have swiftly turned and I can smell the argument we're about to have in the air. "Well, I'm sorry."

"You don't sound sorry."

I pull at my bonds. "Do we have to talk like this?"

He nods. "Yes, I think we do."

I clench my hands into fists. "You should be apologizing to me."

He barks with laughter. "For what?"

My own anger catches flame and I experience an undercurrent of pleasure. It's hard to explain, the luxury of fighting. Of being mad at each other. There was a time where I couldn't even imagine experiencing such a normal couply thing again. But arguments, bickering is part of life that most of us take for granted. And the part of me that almost lost my own, relishes in the safety of arguing, of being human and in love.

"Can I at least have some clothes?" I don't bother to hide the agitation in my voice.

"No." One hard, simple word.

I growl, and blow out an exasperated breath. "You promised not to go easy on me."

He raises a brow. "If I was going easy on you, I'd already be pounding into you."

"That makes no sense. I just don't want you to bring all... all... methodical. Is that so hard to understand?"

He shakes his head, pinches the bridge of his nose and then holds up one finger. "One, I understand you and after all the times I've fucked you, I am well aware that being taken roughly and possessively is your preference. But may I remind you that you did ask me for this, and I'm sorry, but tying someone up is a methodical process. I have to make sure nothing cuts off your circulation, that it doesn't chafe too much against your skin, that you're immobile but not uncomfortable."

Another finger shoots up. "Two, on top of the physical component I have to pay attention to your mental state. I know you hate to hear this, but you were, in fact, traumatized and almost killed. And I don't give a fuck how much you hate it, Layla, I will not risk your emotional wellbeing and go too fast. I *will not* risk you having a panic attack, forced to stand there and watch your eyes grow unfocused and fill with horror as you relive what happened to you, because of something *I* did to you. And if you don't understand that, too fucking bad."

A third finger joins the others. "I know you. I know how you are. You've built this up into some sort of test you have to pass or else you've somehow failed me. You've stubbornly convinced yourself that I'm somehow suffering by being with you, regardless of how many times I tell you otherwise. So forgive me if I don't trust you not to try and push through any discomfort or panic to prove some goddamn point."

The fourth finger rises. "Lastly, I'm not all that into bondage, I prefer my hands on you. I like the feel of my fingers on your wrists. The strain of your muscles against me. I know you've built me up into some sort of sexual god, but the truth is I haven't done anything like this in probably a good five years. Long enough I had to come get lessons from goddamn Brandon. There's about a million things I need to make sure of, keep track of, and watch out for without trying to manage your desire to be taken and consumed. So do you think it's possible to cut me some fucking slack and let me concentrate?"

I can only blink at him, stunned.

Wow. He just had like, a meltdown. He has a list of grievances against me.

Giddy happiness fills my chest and all the sudden I'm fighting the urge to laugh.

Then it dawns on me. Or more smacks me over the head with a two-by-four.

This is what I've been wanting. It wasn't some cathartic bondage sex scene—it's this that I've been craving—blessed normalcy where he's not always so ridiculously understanding.

I take a lot of patience. I understand this. I'm one-hundred-percent positive I'm a complete pain in the ass. Michael has the patience of a saint, and his calm, reasonable understanding is…

well… it's annoying. He's always so damned perfect, so reasonable, and levelheaded. I have no room to be this messy, flawed human when he's so above it all.

Sometimes I need him to be a messy human too.

I sniff. "Well, not quite a sexual god."

He stares at me for several long moments before he laughs. "You are the most frustrating woman on the planet."

"I know." All my agitation drains away. I probably should have communicated this in a more mature fashion, but I honestly didn't know this churned away inside me. I'd become single minded in my determination to put that night behind me. I'd latched on to bondage as a way to prove to him he didn't have to be careful with me anymore. How could I know all I wanted was my boyfriend to get mad at me sometimes? To express his very normal irritation when I'm being unreasonable. It's why I need domination in the first place, it helps clear my mind and focus on what I need. Only it doesn't always work out the way I expected. Obviously. I flutter my lashes at him. "Did you really come to Brandon for lessons?"

I love that he did that. That he felt insecure.

"Yes. The asshole gave me shit the whole time."

I meet his eyes and smile. "I'm sorry."

"You should be." Apparently he's still in the mood to be disgruntled.

"Michael?"

"What, Layla?"

"You did it, you tied me up and I didn't panic." I didn't. It's an accomplishment, just not executed in the way I built it up in my mind.

His gaze narrows. "I suppose that's a point. But it made you aggravated, not wet like I want you."

I bite my lip. "I… um… don't like bondage either."

He shakes his head and blows out a breath. "Then why the hell are we doing this?"

"I stubbornly needed to prove a point." I tilt my head. "But I think what I really needed, what we really needed, is this."

He opens his arms. "And what is *this*?"

"You getting mad at me."

His expression twists in utter confusion and it's adorable. "You want me to be mad at you?"

"Not all the time, but sometimes would be nice." He's still looking at me like I'm insane. I let out a slow breath. "You're a lot of pressure to live with."

His brow furrows. "What?"

I flex my hands, my arms are starting to hurt, my muscles strain. "Would you consider letting me down?"

"Since you asked so nicely." He stands and releases the strap at first one wrist then the other before vigorously rubbing my arms.

"What are you doing?"

He shrugs. "Brandon told me to do it, helps with blood flow."

I giggle. "I don't think I was up there long enough."

"Brat." He pinches me and releases the leather straps before bending and taking care of my ankles.

"Can we agree that this will be our first and last bondage session?"

"Deal." He kisses me, a quick brush of his mouth over mine. "Although I might occasionally want to cuff you."

I have an image of him pounding into me from behind, my hands cuffed at the base of my spine and I shiver. "Deal."

He sits me on the bed and stands over me, arms crossed. "Now what is this about me being hard to live with?"

14.

Jillian

I bury my face in my hands and sob, shaking my head, I whisper, "I'm so, so sorry."

"Sssshhh." Leo kisses my temple. "None of that. You're a good girl, Jillian."

I don't feel good. I feel like I've failed. I was so sure. How could I have been so wrong? "I'm sorry."

He walks around me, and forcibly removes my hands from my face, before kissing my lips with the sweetest of kisses. "That is what a safe word is for, Jilly. You're supposed to use it if it gets too much for you."

Tears track down my cheeks and my chest squeezes so tight my heart might burst. I glance behind me. "I didn't want to disappoint you in front of them."

He brushes his mouth over mine, wraps one arm around my waist, and wipes away my tears with his free hand. "You *never* disappoint me. I know you're upset, and you're not going to understand this, but I'm proud of you. The word is there for

101

a reason. And using it just continues to build the trust between us. Do you understand?"

I shake my head and wave my hand toward the room. "But."

He runs a finger down my cheek. "No buts."

I start to speak, but he stops me. "Hang on."

He leans down and feels under the table.

I have no idea what he's doing, but I stare out into the darkness, wondering how many people are judging me.

The room is deathly quiet. Uncomfortably so.

Suddenly the lights click on, I blink against the harsh brightness, trying to adjust from the shift of focused to dispersed light.

Leo stands back up.

Finally, my eyes adjust and I stare into the room.

I blink. And blink again.

I gasp. The room. It's empty.

My gaze flies to Leo. "How? Did they all leave?"

Leo strokes over my cheek. "They were never here. The room has always been empty."

I'm so confused. My forehead creases. "But, I saw. Heard the opening and closing of the door."

"Brandon." Leo gives me a soft smile. He unhooks me from the chain at my throat and takes my hand. "Come on, there's a couch in the corner. Let's go talk this out."

He helps me off the table. My legs are shaky, with shock and relief.

He walks me over to the couch, where he flicks on a small lamp, and then goes to the wall where a panel resides and the spotlight clicks off. The overhead lights go out and all that's left is the soft glow from the lamp next to me. Intimate and personal, just us. Relief floods through me. Leo returns to the couch, sits down and cuddles me into his lap.

I immediately feel better. This is really all I need. The connection between Leo and me.

He pulls a throw over me and I shiver as his body warms away the coldness clinging to my skin. I lick my lips. "I'm sorry."

"You have nothing to be sorry about. It's important for me to know you trust yourself. You were right to safe word. This is a learning experience for both of us."

"How? Did you know I wouldn't be able to go through with it?" How could he know me that well?

"I didn't." One arm cradles my back and the other big hand cups the swell of my hip. "I wasn't sure how it would go. I knew it was something you were convinced you wanted. I knew you fantasized about it. But it was something so out of the norm of anything we'd done, I didn't feel comfortable trusting you to a room full of strangers. So this was my solution. I figured if it ended up not meeting your expectations, you'd feel relieved you were alone. And if you loved it, next time I'd fill the room and make sure the lights were on without any worry that you'd suffer negative impact."

I curl into him, wrapping my fists into his shirt to keep him close. "Thank you."

"You're welcome." He rubs his hand over my hip. "My first priority is to keep you safe."

I kiss his neck. "I swear I'm the luckiest woman in the world."

He squeezes my thigh. "We still need to talk about this. Since you do like exhibitionism, this will help us figure out where your line is."

I run a finger over his jaw. "And what about your line?"

He smiles. "I won't pretend my line wouldn't have been tested if you loved it. I'm still not sure what I'm comfortable with. My plan was to see how this went and figure out what I could take after."

I meet his gaze. "I didn't love it."

He nods. "Tell me why?"

I try and process out my emotions. Riffle through the million thoughts in my head and start with the easiest. "I didn't like the thought of strangers as much as I thought I would. It was easy to stretch the fantasy of what we've already done, thinking that if I was okay with you occasionally doing something in front of Brandon, that hundreds would only increase the excitement more."

"What do you like when it's Brandon?" His fingers play along the skin of my thigh.

"He's our friend. He's safe. I know he won't touch me. That he won't even probably see me naked." I smile. "Well, at least not all at once."

After that disastrous night at Brandon's, Leo has always been very strategic in what he let's Brandon witness.

He chuckles and tucks my hair behind my ear. "So I think what you're saying is that in order to get into the game, you need to trust the person watching you."

I tilt my head. Thinking. "Yes, that sounds right."

"What about out front. You liked that. I could feel how wet you were, and they were strangers. What was the difference?"

I rest my head against his chest and listen to the steady thump of his heart until I figure out the why. "That was just fun, like a flirty little game where I was making you the star. I think because you'd already told me, and it seemed like everyone else in the place, that you were going to take me to a room, I knew nothing of significance was going to happen there, so I could relax. Flirt, have fun and make people jealous of us."

He laughs. "I see. You want people jealous?"

I grin up at him. "Duh, of course."

"It sounds like, unless you're in front of people you trust, that you like the idea of possibly getting caught over actually getting caught. That you like people knowing what we did, versus them watching us?" He shifts me on his lap, and when my legs slightly part, he circles his fingers over my inner thighs. "Is that fair?"

My breath catches. "Can you give me an example?"

His hand dips lower. "Like that night we all went to dinner and I fucked you in that dark stairwell and made sure everyone knew what I'd done to you when we got back to the table."

All the cold from before evaporates as the heat of his body overtakes me. "Yes, like that."

His fingertips brush over my swollen skin. "Not that I had to tell them, with your just fucked hair, pink cheeks and obscene mouth."

"Yes." I rock into him. "That's exactly what I like."

Then he takes my mouth and sucks me under his spell and everything but him finally fades away.

15.

Ruby

Brandon gave us the grand tour, showing us every nook and cranny of the main space. Apparently, he'd bought the whole building and was planning on converting the top levels to offices of some sort to expand his empire. The place is spectacular, and Brandon is clearly excited about his new venture and it's been a pleasure to listen to him talk. Now Chad and I are sitting comfortably in Brandon's office and I'm relaxed for the first time that evening.

Brandon hands first me, then Chad, a snifter full of brandy. I grin. "Fancy."

From what I understand Brandon comes from very old money and by the looks of this place, he has a taste for the finer things in life.

Brandon laughs, and sits across from where Chad and I rest on a plush leather couch that probably cost more than all my furniture in my tiny studio apartment combined. I run my hands over the material. "This is gorgeous."

"It's imported from Paris." Brandon shrugs. "My designer loves to spend my money."

Chad nods, glancing around the place. "She or he has spent it well."

"She," Brandon says and then winks. "I'm positive she goes over budget so I'll take her over my knee and smack her ass red."

Chad laughs. "I'm sure it's worth the hardship."

"Oh, it is. She's a lovely little redhead with a fiery temper to match."

I flush, the reminder of who these men are, rushing back to me. A slow heat kicks up in my belly and I gulp down the brandy and the stirring of…something at his words.

Brandon tilts his chin at me. "That's a pretty flush on your cheeks."

His words only make my skin heat more. A blush on top of a blush. Kill me now.

Chad turns his attention on me, his blue-eyed gaze speculative.

When I don't say anything, Brandon swirls the amber liquid in his glass and asks, "What are you going to do about that curiosity of yours, Ruby girl?"

I shake my head. "Nothing. I'm not curious. I'm just not used to everyone being so open."

It's true. I come from a family of devout, God-fearing Christians, and growing up sex was a four-letter, forbidden word. They are loving and they mean well, it's just that such things are not discussed. I've mainly gotten over the ultra-conservative upbringing. I share sex details with Layla. Of course, my details are about a million times tamer than hers, but that's not the point. She's my best friend. Brandon and Chad are strangers to me.

"How's that?" Brandon asks. "You're friends with Layla and Jillian and I know for a fact they aren't shy. And this is the twenty-first century. You're a grown, modern woman, surely the mention of sex isn't enough to give you an attack of the vapors."

I wave my hand, mild defensiveness stirring in my chest. "I blushed a little. I hardly had a heart attack. Besides, you weren't talking about sex."

He grins, shrugging. "What's a little spanking among friends?"

I can't help it, the laugh spurts forth, and I shake my head. "You're the worst."

"I know, everyone says so." Brandon raises a brow at Chad. "What do you think? Do you believe her?"

"Yes." Chad's gaze narrows on mine and I resist the urge to squirm under his scrutiny. "And no."

I swat at his arm. "It's true."

Brandon takes a sip of his drink. "You know, Ruby, I'm sure Chad, myself, or both of us together would be happy to give you a little taste. Safely, of course, without any actual S-E-X involved. Don't you agree, Chad?"

The squirming instinct gets the best of me, and I shift in my seat, eyeing the door for my escape. I risk a glance at Chad whose attention is intent on mine.

Slowly, he says, "Definitely."

Now they are making me nervous. Very nervous. Oddly, the image that flashes through my mind is of Chad, not Brandon. His big, tanned hands skimming along my pale, white skin.

I blush even harder and want to bury my face and hide. But I manage to remain composed, despite the heat crawling up my neck. I hold up my hands. "Very nice of you, but I can assure you, that's not necessary."

Brandon grins. "We wouldn't even have to touch you."

"We'd just direct you," Chad adds.

I experience a mixture of terror and arousal. My nipples pull tight and I'm thankful I'm wearing black. I clear my throat. "That's very thoughtful of you, but I'll have to pass. Besides, we're friends and everyone knows what happens when you mix friendship with…" I trail off and look back and forth between them. "Whatever it is you're offering."

Brandon starts to speak, but then his phone goes off, and

he picks it up from the table and sighs. "I have to take care of something. But you guys feel free to stay here and chill."

He gets up and strolls out of the room, leaving an awkward tension in his wake.

I take a sip of my brandy, and it burns down my throat, hitting my stomach and warming me all over. I stare into the glass, watching the play of light ripple along the amber surface.

"I think you're lying," Chad says and my head jerks up.

I blink. "About what?"

He slides his arm along the back of the couch, watching me in that intent way he has. His body is relaxed, his muscles loose, but it's his eyes that tell the story behind the affable, charming good guy. "I think you're more than curious. And I think eventually that curiosity is going to get the better of you."

I should deny this, but as my heart skips a beat, I ask, "Why do you think that?"

He leans forward. "Because you try very hard, but you can't quite hide the longing."

"That's absurd. I am not longing for anything." My voice is shaky and I point to the door, to remind him of our conversation before. "What about what you said out there in the bar? About how you're not going to try and convince me."

"All true. I'm not. And I don't know if it makes your cunt wet."

I gasp at the blunt words. A nervous laugh escapes my lips. "I can assure you it doesn't."

He takes a sip of his drink, still peering at me. "Maybe, maybe not. But I see you wondering if it might."

"Any wondering you sense on my part is merely confusion why anyone would even want such a thing." I'm stating a truth. That is absolutely what I believe.

He shrugs. "Time will tell, but I'll tell you one thing of which I am certain. I've seen the boys you date, and I've paid attention. I can assure you they don't fuck you properly."

Surprise rolls through me and I rear back, gaping at him. I mean to skewer him, but that's not what flies out of my mouth. "Why would you think that?"

"Instinct. Observation." He leans close, and I suck in a breath, taking in his clean, spicy scent. "You date boys masquerading as men. Boys playing at being cool and in control, but aren't. Boys that play games and create drama and want you to chase them in order to validate their self worth."

I can only sit here, frozen. Because clearly he's been paying far too close attention. That's exactly who I date. Exactly the type I fall for, letting them wrap me up in an angsty game that I'll be the one they change for, all the while knowing they'll never give me what I desire. Never give me the kind of love and devotion Michael and Leo give their women.

That Chad sees this so clearly unnerves me. I have to deny. "That's not true."

"Isn't it?" He takes a leisurely sip of his drink.

I shake my head.

"Liar." He meets my gaze, dead-on and unflinching. "Guys like that tend to be too ego driven to know how to make a woman come hard."

"I come." My voice is ripe with indignation. Why am I even entertaining this discussion?

He raises a brow. "With a man?"

Shock bursts through me, vibrating like a clap of thunder. I sputter in a harsh, whispery tone, "I'm not going to dignify that with an answer."

My throat goes dry with fear and a weird panic beats wildly in my chest. He can't possibly know that. *It's a guess.* That's all it is. A stab-in-the-dark guess.

That also happens to be a fact.

I have never been able to have an orgasm with a guy. I can have them by myself. But orgasms and men have always eluded me. I don't know why. No matter how into the guy I am, I don't know how to lose myself. The second we start fooling around I feel like I'm having an out-of-body experience, like I'm watching a movie instead of participating. And not even a good movie sex scene, but an awkward one. When I'm with someone, I can never forget that I'm having sex. That he's watching me. That I have to put on a good performance and be the woman he wants me to be. Experience and age had only made the problem worse, instead of becoming more comfortable, I crawl deeper and deeper into my head.

I remember back in the old days when I shared an apartment with Layla and I'd hear her screaming through the walls as John did god knew what to her. I'd always sit there, stunned, trying to figure out what he could possibly be doing to her that would make her lose control like that.

I've never even had the urge to groan. I mean, I do, because it's expected, but it's timed and choreographed for when he licks my nipples, or plays with my clit, not because I can't contain myself. I've certainly never experienced the hazy, dazed lust I have seen on both Layla's and Jillian's faces.

I'm excellent at faking orgasms though.

I fake orgasms like I'm Meryl Streep up for her twentieth Oscar nomination.

Nobody has ever figured it out—not one guy I've slept with has ever even suspected. So how has Chad? A man that's never touched me? That I didn't think even paid the least bit of attention to me.

It's a guess, Ruby. It's only a guess.

His blue eyes pin me to the spot and suddenly he doesn't seem so harmless. "I'm right."

I shake my head.

His gaze rakes over me. "Ruby, you've never been fucked well in your life."

"Why would you say that to me?" My words are as choked and strained as I feel.

His attention falls first to my lips, and then raises to meet what I'm sure are stunned eyes. "Because you deserve to be."

I should be rejecting every single thing he says. I should be furious. I should rage at him. Slap him. Tell him to mind his own fucking business. Those are all the things a sane person would do, but what scares the hell out of me, what terrifies me, is what I *want* to do.

I want to confess.

I want to tell him the truth.

I want to break down and cry on his shoulder.

I want him to hold me close as I tell him my deepest, darkest secrets.

That there's something wrong with me.

That I fear I'm defective and that I'll never get sex the way everyone else does.

That I've been pretending all this time and I'm so tired.

That I'm scared. Scared I'll go my whole life never feeling the way everyone else takes for granted.

Why do I want to talk to him about things I've never told anyone? That I don't even let myself think about late at night, staring up at my ceiling.

I am wrong about Chad Fellows. He is not harmless. Somehow he's managed to see something I've kept hidden from everyone, including my best friends, and every lover I've had. Without ever touching me. Or really knowing me.

He's dangerous.

I stand up, tugging my skirt down because I suddenly feel naked. I clear my throat. "I should go."

"Ruby," he says, standing and grasping my arm. "Wait."

I need to get out of here. I pull away. "I… Um… I need to go. I, um, forgot someplace I need to be."

"Ruby," he says again.

But I'm already on my way out the door and I don't intend to stop for anyone.

16.

Jillian

Leo pulls away, hand on my breast, his breath as harsh and panting as my own. He bites my lower lip and the sting is like a lightning bolt straight between my legs. "If we're not going to play out your thousand-eyes-upon-you fantasy, we'll have to think of something else. I can't take you to a sex party and just fuck you."

I groan. "But why?" I shift, trying to get closer, my body already restless and aching. I lick into his mouth before whispering against his lips, "You've been denying me all day."

His hand slips between my legs and squeezes my inner thigh. "I think I can make you more greedy." His fingers stroke over my clit, and I'm once again swollen and wet. "I want you mindless and begging." He kisses me. "Unable to form a coherent sentence."

I clutch at his shoulders. "Leo."

He puts his hands on my waist. "Up you go, girl."

"But..." I start to protest, but he gives a sharp look and I go quiet, standing on wobbly legs.

He rises and looks down at me. "Good girl."

I shiver with lust and let out a little moan.

He laughs. "God, I was such an idiot."

I grin up at him. "About what?"

He tugs at a lock of my hair. "All those years we wasted while I was convinced you were a nice, vanilla girl instead of the little submissive slut you are."

"Just think." I lick his lower lip, loving the harsh intake of his breath. "If you'd let me walk away, neither of us would have known. And wouldn't that have been a shame?" I trail my lips over his. "I could have gone my whole life and not had any idea."

There was a time when being called a slut would have filled me with terror, but after a year with Leo my line has changed dramatically. He wants me to be a little slut. For him and only him. And, god, am I.

"That would have been a travesty." He squeezes me tight.

He leads me back to the table and sits me on top of it. When I'm situated he walks behind me and starts in on the laces at my waist. I crane my neck and grin back at him. "I'm glad we waited. Even though I wanted to kill you at the time."

He works his finger under the crisscrossing straps and pulls. "Why's that?"

For a second I don't answer, I just watch him, the concentration in the set of his mouth. The furrow of his brow as he works me out of the corset. His dark, handsome features I know now as well as I know my own. He's a part of me. His life is so entwined in mine we're impossible to separate. "Because as much as I chased you, back then I wouldn't have been ready for you."

He glances up at me. "And now?"

I lean back and kiss him. "And now I am."

"Good." He returns to his task.

"Will you sing for me at our wedding?"

He laughs. "Yes."

I beam. Before I came along Leo hadn't sung since the day

they buried his twin brother in the ground. "Nana and your mom will be so happy."

"What do you want me to sing?"

"I'll let you choose."

He raises a brow. "I'll surprise you."

"I love surprises."

He grins and it's pure evil. "I know. Let's see what we can do about that, shall we?"

The dress pools at my waist. Excitement thrums through my blood. "Yes, please."

He slides his hands under my dress and up my thighs. "Lift."

I do and he pulls the dress free, dropping it to the floor. "Stay."

I give a little salute. "Yes, sir."

Then he sinks down, and licks my clit, and I jump in surprise and then let out a low moan. My head falls back as my fingers tangle in his hair and I arch my hips.

Leo is so talented with his tongue my eyes practically roll into the back of my head.

His lips suck on my swollen flesh as he traces slow circles over the bundle of nerves, driving me mad.

I gasp and my hips become an insistent roll. "Oh, god, yes."

My body quickens.

He bites, gently tugging my skin and I cry out, digging my hands into his hair to push him closer.

My muscles tighten.

The orgasm swells within me.

And then he's gone.

I want to curse him. Want to push his head back down, but I know better than that.

He rises to his feet and I only pant at him in silence.

He points a finger at me. "Stay."

This time, I don't speak.

He walks over and turns off the soft light, and it plunges me into darkness, then the bright spotlight once again turns on. I blink against the bright light, searching for him until he steps into focus.

His lips brush mine and I can taste myself on him, smell the scent of my arousal filling the air. "Just because I'm the only one here, doesn't mean you can't give me a show. Now does it?"

Excited anticipation dances through me. "What does that mean?"

He gives me that sly smirk that says he knows he's got me. I know that look. My stomach dips to my feet. "There's more than one way to be on display."

My heart flips over. "Please no."

"Oh yes, you're going to dance for me." He takes out his phone and starts sliding his thumb over the screen before he raises a brow. "And, Jillian, make it good."

Then the sounds of Def Leppard's "Pour Some Sugar on Me" fills the room, the base pumping through me. I bury my face in my hand and scream. *Why, why, why do I have these exhibitionist tendencies?* "You've got to be kidding me!"

"Nope," he says, that evil grin still in place.

I throw up my hands. "How are you even hooked up to Brandon's sound system?"

"You know I never leave anything to chance, I came last week and got the rundown." He laughs, and tucks my hair behind my ears. "How did you think I knew how to work all the lights?"

"Electronic genius?"

He gives me his stern-eyed look. "Flattery will only get you another song. So I suggest you get to it."

Oh, God, help me. "I don't want to, it's embarrassing. I'm naked."

"There isn't an inch of your body I haven't seen in every single possible position and angle." He twines his fingers through my hair. "You don't have to, of course. You always have choices. So let me lay them out for you. Choice number one, you give me the show you've been begging for all night, get your pussy smacked, your brains fucked out and multiple orgasms. Choice two, we go home, put on some sweatpants and watch a movie. Orgasms not included. Your choice, girl."

I blink at him, staring at him as the song thumps through the speakers before I say, "You are the meanest man in the world."

The sad thing is, this is exactly the kind of thing I love to hate. The twisting of the knife, it's the most evil, delicious, wonderful thing in the entire world.

"I know." His tone is entirely too satisfied.

"You won't be able to resist me," I challenge. The surge of adrenaline making my blood pump hard and my brain turn stupid.

"I won't have to. I'll jerk off and come all over you." He laughs and chucks me under the chin. "Unlike you, I can have as many orgasms as I want."

I hate him.

I love him.

Because under all the stress of having to put on a sexy, naked dance for my fiancé, I'm so damned turned on I could scream in frustration. The man knows me far, far, far too well.

He licks my lower lip. "It won't be as good as coming in that hot, wet cunt of yours, but it will do until you give me what I want."

The song flips over to "99 Problems" by Hugo. He raises a brow. "What's it going to be?"

I won't be able to break him. Not in this. Because he knows how that secret part of me gets off on this.

I nod.

"Good girl." His fingers tighten in my hair. "Go back and remember what it was like when you were desperate to seduce me. Don't tell me you never danced for me, and only me before."

I swallow. A memory of us at a party. The music a slow beat, Leo's eyes hot and hungry on me. I'd worked it.

He'd resisted me then.

He won't resist me now.

Back then I'd been wearing a slinky black dress and tonight I'm wearing nothing but high heels. I give him a pout. "But there's no stripper pole."

"You can use me instead." He pulls me off the table and sits on it. "Seduce me and see where it gets you."

I can feel it. That thing I've been searching for since I stepped into this room. Where the rest of the world melts away and it's all about what Leo wants.

He pulls out his phone, taps on the screen until "Pour Some Sugar on Me" comes back on.

I arch my brow. "Really? The most clichéd song in the world?"

He laughs, and puts his phone on the table and leans back on it. "Jilly, there's not a man alive that hasn't fantasized about a girl dancing to this song just for him."

He pushes a button on his phone and it starts from the beginning again. "I suggest you stop stalling and get a move on."

And I do.

I let everything melt away.

With my eyes on him I let my hips find the rhythm of the song. I let my body sway to the music, getting lost in the bass, the pounding thrust of the lyrics.

I dance closer to him, then back.

Retreating and pushing forward as his eyes never leave me. His gaze predatory and possessive. Hot. He's in a claiming mood; I can see it in his expression. When this song is over, my wait will be over too.

On my next advance, I put my hands on his knees and dip down before rolling up over him. Pleased when I hear the low groan, and see his knuckles whiten.

I climb up him, pressing close, sliding my breasts along his chest and he growls, low in his throat.

I straddle him, kneeling over him and preform the sluttiest, dirtiest grinding lap dance in the history of lap dances, rubbing my bare pussy over his erection still covered by his pants.

I can feel how hard he is. How much he wants me.

It strains and pulses the air.

The fabric of his pants is a delicious, excruciating tease but

I don't stop, don't let up.

I whip my hair, arch my back and slither over him.

"Christ," he mutters and grips the edges of the table.

The song ends and he's on me.

He takes my mouth in a hard, brutal kiss that steals my breath and whatever is left of my sanity.

His hands are everywhere.

He pulls viciously at my nipples and I cry out. Then he's lifting us, turning and slamming me down on the table.

I'm panting.

Gasping for air.

My body is on fire.

I claw at his shirt, but he just unzips his pants and impales me.

At the force of his entry I keen, arching up off the table. "Leo. Fuck."

He grips my hips and pounds into me, his expression hard and demanding.

He's ruthless.

He thrusts, his fingers digging into my skin where I'm sure to have bruises.

He pulls out. Growls. And slaps me, full on the clit.

I scream. "I'm going to come."

"No." He's Leo, unleashed. A cruel, selfish bastard that will wring every last bit of pleasure from my body before he's satisfied.

He does it again.

And again.

I arch up. It hurts, but, oh my god, it feels so good.

It's like something has broken between us.

He starts fucking me again.

Pounding harder into me.

Thrusting faster.

Just as I'm about to come he rips away.

And slaps me full on the pussy and I swear I see stars. "I can't…"

"No." He slams into me.

Harder. Faster. Unrelenting.

"Leo?" I cry out his name.

"Now." His voice is vicious and harsh.

He thrusts into me while he slams my hips down with his hands and that's all it takes. I'm coming so hard my vision blurs as it rolls through my body. I shudder, quake and lose myself in the sheer bliss of him.

I have no idea how long we stay like that but it feels like forever as we melt together boneless and satiated. Finally, he raises his head and looks at me before brushing my hair off my face. He smiles. "You are going to be doing that all the time."

"So you liked it?"

He kisses me. "Hot as hell."

I laugh. "Do I have to dance to 'Pour Some Sugar on Me'?"

"Fuck yes."

I smile and close my eyes. We'll see. Not worth arguing about now.

His mouth skims up my jaw. "Jilly?"

"Yes?" I might never move again.

"I can't wait to marry you."

I grin. "It's going to be epic."

"It is." His voice is soft and sweet, his tone just for me. "I love you so damn much."

"I love you too." I kiss his lips. Brush my hand over his cheek. "Happy Valentine's Day."

"Happy Valentine's Day."

He straightens. "There's a million things I need to do to you tonight."

"Then we'd better get started."

He runs his thumb over my lower lip. "At home."

Home. With Leo. The only place that really matters to me. "Home is definitely in order."

"Oh, and, Jillian?" His expression turns wicked and my heart skips a beat.

"Yes?"

"Don't think I've forgotten about the belt."

I sigh in an exaggerated pout. Of course he hasn't. Bless his deviant heart.

17.

Layla

We sit down on the bed, hands clasped. Michael squeezes my fingers. "Start talking, Layla."

I blow out a hard breath and gather my thoughts. "You're right. I did make this into a pass/ fail. I think I thought if I could conquer this last little bit it would make me normal again."

It's a struggle of mine. To feel normal.

"I've told you before, sugar, you're never going to be normal. And that's not a bad thing."

I nod. "I know. But... I want to be. You know?"

Another squeeze. "I know."

I nibble on my bottom lip. "In my head, my idea was if I was able to do this, you would be able to finally be yourself around me."

He jerks his head toward me, brows furrowed. "I am myself around you."

"So, what you're saying is, you're perfect?" I wrinkle my

nose.

He laughs. "Where do you get these ideas?"

I blow out a breath. "I'm serious. Do you know how hard it is? To feel all crazy, irrational and messy when you're all calm and reasonable? It makes me feel like I never get to you. I'm one big mess of flaws and faults and you're just… well, you. Unflappable."

He sighs and runs his fingers through his hair. "Layla, what am I going to do with you?"

"I don't know." My stomach clenches. "I worry. You know?"

"About what?"

He's not going to like it, but I trudge on. "That someday, you'll get tired of all my crazy and decide to find an easier girl to love."

His jaw hardens, and a flash of anger passes over his face. "Don't you have any fucking idea how much I love you?"

"I know you love me. I just don't know how to be perfect for you."

He lets go of my hand and stands, and then starts pacing around the room, clearly agitated. "I don't want you perfect. Even when you're driving me insane."

I motion with my hand. "Yes, more of this."

He stops, and just stares at me for several long beats before he takes a breath. "Here's the thing, if I was crazy, you couldn't handle it."

I vault off the bed and throw my hands in the air. "That's what I'm talking about though. That's exactly it. I *can* handle it. I'm tired of you acting like I can't. I want all of you, not just the part you think I'm okay with. Is that so hard to understand?"

"You are twisting my words."

"Then what are you trying to say?"

"What you need, who you are requires someone with a long fuse. You might hate it, but you wouldn't last two seconds with someone that was messy and irrational. You need an anchor."

I pick up my dress from the floor and slip it on, not asking for permission. When I straighten, covered now, a muscle in his jaw jumps. Before he can say anything about breaking the rules I say, "Yeah, I get that, Michael. But I'm not talking about me. I'm talking about you. We talk ad nauseam about what I need. My point is what do *you* need. And how can I begin to fulfill those needs if I don't even know what they are?"

He crosses his arms over his chest. "So you're saying you don't know me?"

I screech and throw up my hands. "No! I'm saying I don't want our entire relationship to be about managing my needs. I'm saying sometimes it's okay to get pissed at me because I'm being a bitch. That it's okay to get sick of me because I'm too moody, or I'm crying for no reason. Or be aggravated because I'm having a panic attack and you just want to kick back with a beer after work and don't feel like dealing with it. I'm saying it's okay to be human."

"I'm human, Layla."

"If you feel those things, I don't know it, because I never see them. Tonight was the first time you actually ever communicated your frustration with me." My throat gets tight. "And I need that too."

"That's not true, Layla."

"It is!" I insist, stomping my foot for good measure. "Michael, think about it from my perspective. When you were shot, and lying in the hospital bed I left you. That was a shitty fucking thing to do and when I came back, you were forgiving."

One dark brow rose up his forehead. "I was forgiving because I knew you were going to leave and I knew you were going to come back."

"So what?" I shake my head at him. "It was still a shitty thing to do."

"Yeah, it was." He shrugs one big shoulder. "But it wasn't because you are a shitty person, it's because you were scared."

"I know," I say, my voice softens. "And you can still be mad at me."

"So you want me to be mad at you?"

"I want you to be furious with me if that's how you feel."

It seems like a myriad of emotions pass over his face before he finally steps toward me. "You're right."

I blink. "I am?"

He nods. "Sometimes I force myself to cool off before I deal with you because there's a part of me that is always worried you have one step out the door."

My heart swells and my chest grows tight. "I don't. I know I did for a long time, but I don't. You've conquered me."

"I know that here." He touches his temple. "But sometimes I still worry about it. Or I worry something will happen to me and you'll leave again."

I gulp, and swallow down my emotions. "I worry every day something will happen to you, but I don't let it stop me. I'm all in. Both feet and my whole body. I can't live without you, how can I leave?"

He opens his mouth to speak, but then stops, shakes his head and starts again. "Here's what I need."

I pin my gaze on him. "I'm listening."

He steps toward me and his hand curls behind my neck. As always the chemistry that burns between us flares to greedy life. It's a hot tangible thing, stronger today than that night I first met him. It's a bond so strong, and so deep it's exclusive only to him.

His fingers tangle in my hair. "I need to be your rock. I need to be that one person in your life you cling to."

I nod, some of my rigid muscles loosening.

"I need you to push me past my patience sometimes."

"Mission accomplished." I smile.

He smiles back. "Indeed. Believe it or not, I need your messiness because how boring would I be without it?"

I put my hand on his arm. "There's not a woman alive that would think you were boring."

"I don't care about them, I care about you."

We move a little, closing the inches that still separate us.

"What else?" I ask.

"I need your submission. And your devotion."

"You have those."

He swallows and the cords in his neck work and I know he's struggling with something he doesn't want to say.

I squeeze his arm. "Tell me, please."

His expression twists. "I don't know how to communicate to you how much I love you, how much I need you. I wish you could see inside me so you would understand. I have never even come close to loving anyone the way I love you and I know I have to share that with John and I accept that, but…" He trails off and looks away.

Suddenly, I get it. The fog clears and I understand. That feeling I get, that he's holding back, it's not about sex as I assumed. It's about fearing that if he pushes me the wrong way he won't be able to live up to the expectations set by a dead man.

And just like that I know what needs to be done.

"Michael, sit down." I step away from him and point to the bed. "Please."

His face is pinched with worry and I can tell he thinks he's said the wrong thing. With a wary glance he sits.

I straddle him, and his arms go around me, his big hands settling on my hips.

"Look at me," I say, using words he's said to me a thousand times.

He does, and I can tell he wants to protest the sudden shift of power but he remains silent.

I cup his cheek. "I'm going to tell you something, and I'm only going to say it once, so I hope you're really listening."

"I am. But—"

I cut him off. "No, just listen."

"All right."

My throat is tight and I clear it. "I don't feel the same way about you that I felt about John."

"Layla, this isn't necessary. I understand. I don't want—"

I kiss him. "Just listen to me."

"I—" he begins again.

I shake my head. "Listen. You don't have to justify your feelings to me. I loved him. He was comfort to me. Like a safe, warm blanket I could wrap around myself. We had a great relationship, and we had so much fun together. If he were alive I'm positive we'd be living a nice, happy life." Michael's shoulders bunch and flex under my fingers and I can feel his stress. I press my mouth to his in a soothing gesture before I continue. "But the truth is, as much as I loved him, it wasn't like it is with you. Not better or worse, but different. You and I have something unique. The way I want you is unmatched. It's like the second I laid eyes on you every cell in my body woke up."

"You don't have to do this," he says and his voice is strained.

I don't stop. Because I understand him, he doesn't want to feel competitive with John, but he is showing me he's human. I owe him this peace, because it's true. *This* is what I need to do for him. It's something I can give him, after everything he's given me. And he deserves to know how important he is to me, how essential.

I run my thumb over his strong jaw. "I know I don't have to but I want to. I think the difference is, I loved him with the heart of a girl. And I love you with the heart of a woman. The way it is between us, sometimes I'm afraid it will swallow me whole. That I'll burn up with it. Sometimes when we're out, and we're with our friends, all I can think about is when I can have your cock. How soon you'll fuck me and make me whole. It's like a preoccupation. When we're sitting on the couch in our sweatpants, eating takeout, it should be comfortable. And it is. But it's also like there's electricity sparking the air between us. It wasn't like that with John."

His muscles relax under my hands. "So you're obsessed with me?"

I rock against his erection that will be in me soon enough. "Totally."

"You know I'm just as obsessed." His fingers squeeze my hips.

"Are you?"

He yanks me down, grinding his hard cock against my soft, swollen center. "What do you think?"

I lean down and whisper in his ear, "I think I'm the luckiest woman in the world."

He groans, hot against my skin. Before he stills me. "I'm sorry."

"I'm sorry too." My mouth settles on his and our tongues entwine, but before I get lost, I pull away because I want to make sure he understands. "You're not sharing me. I am all yours."

He looks guilty. Conflicted. Because, at his core, he's a good guy with a hero complex that doesn't want to feel anything as petty as jealousy over a dead man.

I know just the thing to ease his mind about that one. I grin and lean back. "You do know you're a better person than me, don't you?"

"No, I'm not."

"Ha. Trust me, you're a lot more understanding than I am. Because believe me, if you had a dead fiancée, it wouldn't matter how good she was to you, I'd hate her. I'd annoy you with questions and make you do a compare and contrast between us. Even then I still wouldn't be satisfied, and I'd make you tell me all sorts of terrible things about her."

He laughs before shrugging. "That doesn't sound unreasonable."

I tilt my head as though pondering. "All right, let me think."

"Not necessary. I don't want you to say anything bad about him."

"No, no, I want to." I can think of John now and it's not a big gaping hole. I can remember the good things about him, and the bad with fondness, instead of grief. I wrinkle my nose. "Well, he was kind of a slob. He used to leave his socks on the floor, like right next to the hamper."

His muscles relax under me. "That is annoying."

"It was. And he would somehow manage never to empty

the dishwasher."

"That's not so bad."

"That's because you hate emptying the dishwasher too."

"Yeah, I do."

I give him a sly look and glance back and forth, as though someone might be watching us. "And he let me top from the bottom, like, all the time."

Michael laughs. "Now *that* is a crime."

"It was." I give him a pout. "You never let me. Not even once."

"You wouldn't like it if I did."

"You're right. I wouldn't. Now. You have certainly refined my perception of dominance."

"Is that good?" His expression turns curious.

"Very good." I rock against him. "The best."

His gaze locks with mine, and everything inside me stills. He runs his hands up and down my back. "Thank you, Layla."

"You're welcome."

"I think you're right, we needed to have the conversation." He shakes his head. "I didn't know. And I'll try, okay."

"That's all I ask. I'm not asking you to change your personality. But it's okay to get mad at me." I grip his jaw in my hand. "I promise, I'm not going anywhere."

"You promise?"

"You have my word."

Our lips meet, and our mouths turn instantly frantic, taking on a desperate edge that fuels our interactions. The insatiable desire he evokes in me. A gnawing hunger. His tongue sweeps inside, filling me, claiming me.

He lowers us to the bed and I tumble on top of him before he turns me over and I'm trapped under him. He pulls away and brushes my hair back before staring down at me. "So beautiful."

I touch my fingers to his face. "You too."

"I know you have a hard time believing this, but you are the best thing that ever happened to me. My most precious possession."

He means it. I know this deep down in the pit of my stomach. "And you're mine."

"Now I'm going to fuck you. Own your body."

My thighs tighten around his hips and I arch. "Yes."

He moves, levering up and kneeling before reaching for the straps of my dress and peeling them down my body. I lift up, and he rids me of the silky fabric before stripping off his shirt, and unbuckling his belt. Slowly he pulls it from the loops, like he's giving me my own private show. With deliberate movements he unbuttons and unzips his pants and they slip down, displaying the magnificent cut of his lean hips and flat stomach.

My mouth waters. I can barely believe he's mine.

He settles on top of me, and I run my hands down his muscled back, loving the tense and flex as I touch him. He kisses me, slow and deep, unrestrained. The ghost of my dead fiancé evaporates, leaving nothing but Michael and me.

As it should be. As I want it to be. But most important, as I need it to be.

Michael is my life now. My priority. My love.

His mouth slants, and our kiss grows hungry.

He strums over my nipple, plucking at the hard peak, rolling and pinching and pulling until I moan into him.

He groans and rears back. "I want to take this slow." He shucks his pants the rest of the way down, taking his underwear along with him until he's blissfully naked. "But I need you too much right now."

My body keens at his words. Because I want him to need me as much as I need him, and tonight, it finally sinks in that he truly does. That he is as lost without me as I am without him. I lift my hips in offering. "Please."

He growls and climbs up my body, kissing a trail in his wake. "I'm going to fuck your throat."

I shudder. I love when he just takes what he wants. When he uses me for his pleasure.

I part my lips, and wait. He straddles my head, and braces himself on the headboard before pushing his straining cock past my lips.

His thick erection presses deep into my mouth and I lie there, letting him do what he will. He doesn't want performance. He wants surrender. And I'll give him nothing less. He fills my throat, cutting off my air supply before he stills. I relax my throat around him, fighting against my gag reflex. I rest my fingers on his thighs, and close my eyes, willing and accepting.

He pulls back and then thrusts forward, stretching me to maximum capacity.

He lets loose a low, guttural curse, and retreats, only to advance once again.

Over and over.

I surrender to him, completely, letting my mouth and throat communicate the depth of my love for him.

He pulls back, and pops from my lips before he moves down my body to look at me. I shiver with lust, recognizing that feral look in his eyes.

He moves between my legs, grips my hips, and slams into me, leaving me gasping and panting. He covers me. Takes my wrists and clasps them in his strong hands, squeezing until I'm confined under him. Unable to do anything, but take his hard, brutal thrusting.

I'm captured. And there's nowhere else I'd rather be in this world.

He growls, low in my ear. "Nothing feels as good as you tight around me."

"Yes." My body catches fire as he moves ruthlessly inside me.

"Mine." The word is harsh.

"Always," I pant back.

The orgasm barrels fast upon me. I clench my fingers, fighting the release, not ready for it to end. Because I feel it. It finally sinks in that there's no barrier between us.

He's fucking me like I'm his salvation.

"Michael, god, Michael." I want to claw at his back, but I can't because he's restrained me so completely I can only move my hips in a hard, rocking rhythm that matches his own.

"That's right, sugar, I want you to come hard on my cock." His voice is a low rumble that breaks me.

The climax explodes through me, shaking my whole body, stunning me silent. It rolls and crashes over me, going on and on and on.

I never want it to end. And I work my hips harder and harder into him. Wanting somehow to meld him to me.

Another orgasm crests and I cry out, arching as my muscles clamp around him, ripping his own shuddering climax from him.

We move like that, not wanting to break the connection for endless minutes, surging in tiny, pulsing shock waves of pleasure.

I don't know how much time passes as we drift along in a cloud of pure bliss, but he finally stirs, rising to his elbows to look down at me.

He brushes my mouth with his. "There's something else I need."

"Anything." I'm so content I would promise him the entire universe if I could deliver.

He whispers, "I need permanent. I need *you* to be permanent."

My heart gives a hard thump against my chest. "I am."

He rolls away and leaves the bed. "Stay here."

I close my eyes. As though I could even move. As if I'd go anywhere without him.

I hear him rummaging around, but I'm too lazy to see what he's doing. Too boneless to do anything but lie here and wait for him to return.

He climbs onto the bed and my lashes flutter but he says, "No, keep your eyes closed."

I relax back into the bed.

He places something on the dip between my ribs, something small, like a box.

My belly does a strange little flip. I stir. But he presses me back down. "Michael?"

He strokes my hair. "Now I want you to listen. Since the day I met you, I knew you were it for me. You are the most challenging, frustrating, fascinating and compelling woman I have ever met. And I'm not willing to be without you."

My throat closes over and I start to tremble.

"I love you and want us to have a life together." He leans down and brushes his lips over mine. "Open your eyes."

All traces of sleepiness is gone and my lids snap open. He's smiling down at me.

There is a jeweler's box resting where my ribs dip. Open, a huge emerald-cut platinum ring is resting in the center.

Tears immediately fill my eyes and spill onto my cheeks. Shocked, I look up at him.

He brushes the tears away, a gesture he's done a thousand times since he's known me, since the first night I met him. But now, it's tears of happiness. Tears of joy. He licks his tongue over my bottom lip. "So, Layla Hunter, girl of my dreams, love of my life. Will you marry me?"

I swallow hard. I'd never thought I'd do this again, I'm terrified, I'm elated and overwhelmed. But I want it. I have never wanted anything more in my entire life. I nod and choke out, "Yes, Michael."

He takes the ring box from my stomach, and plucks the diamond from the center where it was resting. "Give me your hand."

I raise my hand and he slips the ring over my finger.

It's a perfect fit. "Michael."

I'm incapable of speech.

I look down at my hand, now adorned with this incredible ring. It shines in the light, an indestructible stone.

"Do you like it?" he asks.

I finally find my voice. "Are you kidding?" I shift just to watch it sparkle. "It's the most beautiful ring I've ever seen. But, how…" I trail off. The stone is at least two carats, maybe even more, and a bright white color shows its high quality. Rings like this cost a fortune and Michael is a homicide detective.

He grins at me. "The stone was my grandma's. She gave it to my mom with explicit instructions that it was to be given to me if I found a woman worthy of it. I did. Apparently, it's a tradition and one day you're supposed to pass it down to your first-born grandchild."

And that makes it all the more special. Because it's an heirloom and his family trusts me to have it. "I will treasure it always."

"It's a good thing I said something to my mom—I wasn't going to tell anyone—but at the last minute I wanted a female perspective on the setting. Out went the very respectable one carat stone and in went this. But everything else is the same." He rubs a hand over my stomach. "I figure we can use the money I saved for furniture when we get a bigger place."

We'd been talking about it—feeling his condo was getting too small—and I'd recently put my place on the market. It had been a bittersweet day.

Once I'd dreamed of suburbia, but I'd abandoned those notions. Because of his job Michael has to live in the city of Chicago. We talked about moving to one of those areas on the outer limits, pressed up against the suburbs where we could have a house and a yard for Belle, but it turns out I'm a city girl at heart.

I like the chaos of it, of being in the heart of things, even when it sucks to get your groceries because of traffic. Between the sales of both our places, we'll be able to get a nice, townhouse with at least three bedrooms that will be perfect.

For at least a while until we decide it's time to have kids. A small smile lifts my lips. Look at me, planning a future. "Sounds perfect."

"I love you, Layla." He kisses me and I cling to him for dear life, this man who's brought me back from the dead and made me complete.

When he pulls back, I say, "I love you too."

And I do, so, so much. I start to laugh.

"What?" He shakes his head at me.

"I just got engaged on Valentine's day."

"You did." He leans back and props himself up against a pillow and headboard.

"That's the most normal thing in the world."

He laughs. "I suppose that's true, although I'm guessing we shouldn't tell our parents that I asked you at a BDSM sex party."

I shrug. "Well, god, we're not completely boring."

He laughs again.

I raise my brow. "Did you ask my dad?"

"Of course I did."

My fiancé, so traditional, when he's not being all dominating and bossy. "What did he say?"

His expression turns serious. "He said he thanked God every day you found love again. And your mom cried."

"I'm thankful every day too."

"Me too, sugar."

That nickname he gave me the night we met when I refused to tell him my name never fails to make me a little weak in the knees. I bite my lip.

He narrows his gaze. "What?"

I sit up and bounce on the bed. "Is it wrong I want to be a total girl right now and go screaming to my friends that I'm engaged."

His expression fills with amusement. "Sounds reasonable."

I giggle. "Can we buy a *Bride* magazine on the way home?"

"Anything you want, Layla, it's yours." He grins. "As long as you ask permission first."

"Deal." And just like that I realize I've gotten my wish. My secret longing.

Here I am, a normal girl, happy and engaged. I get to pick out placemats and china patterns. I get to try on wedding dresses. I get to drive everyone crazy talking about wedding plans.

I have everything I have ever wanted, with just the right amount of kinky, twists to keep life interesting.

18.

Ruby

I take off, forcing myself not to run. Running away from Chad will only make him think he's right about me. Which he is, but I don't want him to know it.

Unfortunately, not running allows him to catch up to me. He grasps me around the arm and hauls me back, pushing me against the wall.

"What?" I snap at him.

His hold gentles. "Hey. Hold on."

I shake my head. "Please. I just want to go home."

"I'm sorry." His voice is deep and soothing as his expression searches mine.

"Don't be." I wave my free hand. "It's not a big deal, I am tired and ready to go to bed is all. I've had enough sex party for the night."

His hand is heavy on my arm, too warm against my skin. I want to rip it away but that would be telling. And I don't want him to see any more than he has.

His gaze dips to my mouth. "I shouldn't have said that to you. I apologize. I don't know you, and shouldn't presume."

See, it was a guess. It doesn't mean anything. He didn't see anything.

The smart thing to do here is nod, accept his apology and brush it off. Never to be spoken of, or thought of, again. And when I open my mouth that's my intention, but my words don't cooperate. "But that's still what you think?"

Again he searches my expression, clearly looking for something that eludes me. "What would you like me to say here, Ruby? Tell me."

His tone has that certain something I've heard in Leo's and Michael's voices. Something that stills me. I shake my head. "I don't know. The truth?"

"It is what I think." His hand falls away.

I find I miss it. It felt good on my skin, even though I wanted him to stay away. I'm a mess, but I don't know how to stop my spiral. "Why?"

He shrugs. "I just have that feeling, call it instinct."

I lick my lips. "Is it because I'm not sexy like Layla and Jillian?"

Why did I say that? Why did I even think it? I'm plenty good looking. I know for a fact I'm pretty, but I didn't use the word pretty. I used the word sexy.

And that's what tonight has brought home to me. Why I have felt so out of sorts, jealous of my best friend, jealous of the way her man looks at her. There's a part of me that believes I'll never have what Layla or Jillian have, because I lack that certain spark, that certain effortless sexiness that seems to come so natural to them.

Chad's blue eyes narrow. "Why do you think you're not sexy?"

I shrug. What can I possibly say? "I was wondering if that's it?"

He steps close to me, and cups my jaw, tilting my head up to meet his gaze. His eyes have darkened and his expression is intense and serious. "You're sexy, Ruby. You're actually pretty fucking gorgeous. You just fight it too hard."

My throat is tight. A part of me wants nothing more than to end this conversation, but I find I can't. Because another part of me wants to understand what he sees. I don't know why. It's like a compulsion. "Why do you think that?"

"You tell me." His thumb brushes over the line of my jaw.

"I don't know." My words are soft, barely above a whisper.

"Am I right?"

I close my eyes and nod.

"I—"

I don't know what the rest of his sentence is because Layla screams my name, "Ruubbyy!"

My lids fly open and Chad's hand drops away. He steps back just as Layla comes flying down the hall in her filmy white dress.

I straighten from the wall. "What's wrong?"

"Nothing." She tackles me, and I see Michael from behind her, watching with that love-soaked affection on his face. She laughs. "I'm engaged."

My heart drops into my stomach and my chest twists tight.

I hate myself for it.

I plaster on my hugest smile and squeal. "Oh my god, Laylay! Congratulations."

She pulls away from me and her expression is filled with an excitement that lights up her whole face. She holds out her left hand. "Look!"

I grasp her fingers and stare down at a gorgeous ring. It's platinum and classic, and the huge emerald-cut stone is set high. It's one of the prettiest things I've ever seen and exactly right for Layla. The smile on my face is so wide it hurts, but on the inside a part of me is dying.

I'm a horrible friend.

"Wow. That is a serious ring." I look at Michael, this darkly gorgeous, intense man that stole my best friend's heart. "Good job."

He just shrugs and grins at Layla, shaking his head.

I will be forever grateful for everything he's done for her.

She's the girl she used to be and so, so much more. And I know that's because of him. Because he loved her so much, he wouldn't leave, no matter how hard she tried to push him away.

They deserve every ounce of happiness and I will not begrudge them that because of my own petty issues. As Layla hugs Chad, I walk over to Michael and wrap my arms around him. I kiss his cheeks and feel my eyes tear up. I whisper in his ear, "Thank you for making her so happy."

He squeezes me tight and says, "I promise she means everything to me."

There's no doubt in my mind. "I know."

As he releases me, Jillian and Leo appear, and then there's more screaming and hugging, and back slapping.

Jillian grabs Layla and the two of them bounce around in their little dresses, looking like goddesses and little girls all at the same time.

Jillian laughs. "We're going to be sisters-in-law!"

"We are!" Layla screeches back.

Leo and Michael kind of roll their eyes at each other, but the big goofy smiles on their faces give them away.

Brandon comes up, and beckons us. "I have four bottles of Dom chilling for just this thing."

Layla glances at Michael. "Did you tell him?"

"I wanted to make sure you got a proper engagement party."

Michael always thinks of everything.

Layla bounds over to him, whispers something in his ear that has his arms coming around her, and then she's kissing him. A raw, dirty, hungry kiss that makes me blush and yearn. Uncomfortable and longing.

I'm so, so happy for her. I promise you I am.

This pit in my stomach, the heaviness in my chest, that's about me. Not her.

Brandon gestures into the open bar, crowded now since we left. "I have a place reserved. Let's celebrate."

Arm in arm Layla and Michael push forward, and just as I

go to follow, Chad's hand grips my arm again. "Hey, we should talk."

I make sure I have the most brilliant smile on my face. "It's a celebration, it's a good night. Let's just forget everything."

He hesitates, his fingers tightening on my arm fractionally before he releases me. "All right."

I'm relieved he's not pushing me, because if he did, I think I'd break.

And that's not possible. I need to be happy for Layla and Michael.

I need to sever this weird intimacy between Chad and me.

"Time to celebrate." I square my shoulders and trudge on.

I'll think later. Alone in bed.

But for now I'll be happy. Or at least pretend. Nobody will know.

I glance at Chad, who's watching me with that certain expression.

Except him.

19.

It's late. And we are all drunk on too much champagne.

Ruby made an excuse, saying she had to get up early, and called an Uber. She stumbled out of the club, and as covertly as I could, I excused myself and followed her.

I'm not sure why I'm not letting this go. I should.

Ruby is not my type. I like women like me. Girl-next-door types. Uncomplicated. Everything Ruby is not. But there is something about her that calls to me.

Something about her I can't let go.

I'm not sure if it's even attraction. I wasn't lying when I told her she was gorgeous earlier, because she absolutely is. Like Snow White, with her red lips, black hair, blue eyes and pale ivory skin. She also has a body that will not quit, but rocker girls aren't really my scene.

And Ruby has issues. Of that I'm certain.

I don't have the time or inclination to deal with issues.

But I'm still following her.

I find her outside, leaning against the brick of the building, her eyes closed.

I shove my hands in my pockets and walk over to her. "Hey."

Her thick lashes flutter open. "Hey."

I look at her mouth. Her parents were right to name her Ruby. The name matches her lips. "How drunk are you?" I'm not going to lie, my own words slur a bit.

"Pretty drunk," she says, her voice unsteady.

That's what I thought. I have no business being alone with her. I push my hands deeper into my pockets. I won't touch her. "Are you okay?"

She looks at me. Her eyes a brilliant, watery blue. "I think I'm going to cry."

"Go ahead." I nod my reassurance. I don't get all worked up over tears the way normal men do. Being dominant, making a woman cry, whether it's from too many orgasms or forcing her to release emotions she's pent-up inside, comes with the territory. "I can be your shoulder if that's what you need."

One lone tear tracks down her cheek. "You would?" Her tone takes on a pleading note.

Fuck. I hold out my arms and she steps into them. Her head rests on my chest, her soft, shiny, shoulder-length hair brushing the underside of my chin. I wrap her up in my embrace, and she starts to shake.

I say nothing. I just let her have it out.

She cries, long and hard, her tears wetting my shirt as she clutches at me like I'm her lifeline in the fiercest of storms. She hiccups against me. "I'm a terrible person."

I rub her back. "No, you're not. It's just been a rough night."

I'm the only one that saw her face when Layla announced she was engaged. She put on an excellent show. But I saw her expression twist in pain while she hugged Layla. I know she's happy for her friend, but she's clearly going through some sort of internal crisis she's trying to hide from the world. Hide from herself. And it's just gotten too much for her. She's a good actress—too good—but for some reason I see through it.

The Uber car pulls up and I'm about to tell her, but she fists my shirt. "Please don't tell anyone."

I signal to the driver that it will be a minute then return back to her.

"I won't." I hug her tighter and she trembles against me. "Your secrets are safe with me."

She cries some more and then when she finally seems to settle she looks up at me with her tragic, tear-stained face. "You're right."

"About what?" Although I know.

She blinks. "I've never had an orgasm with a man."

I nod. "I know."

"How?"

The truth is, I don't know how. I just do. It's written in her face. In the confusion in her eyes. The etch of unease at the corners of her ruby lips. The flush of pink across her cheeks. She wants to pretend, wants it not to be so, but Ruby is not a woman comfortable with sex. She's not easy in her sexuality.

I'd stake money that she has never had a fulfilling sexual experience with a man. There's just too much bewilderment for there to be any other option.

I don't think she's ready to hear all those things yet.

She's still waiting for me to answer. I wipe the wetness from her cheek and it smears some of her mascara, making her look even more tragically beautiful. "It was an educated guess."

"Nobody has ever guessed."

I run my finger over her jaw. "Then the men you've been with don't pay nearly enough attention."

Her gaze skirts to my mouth and I can feel her coil tight, readying herself.

I know what she wants, somehow to lose herself in me, but that's not going to happen. I'm drunk. She's drunk. Emotions are too high.

I rub my thumb over her lower lip and she parts on a gasp. "Your car is here."

"Oh," she says in a breathy lost voice that makes me hard.

"You need to go."

An array of emotion plays out over her face, but she nods. "Okay."

I hold out my hand. "Give me your phone."

She pulls it out of her pocket and gives it to me without protest.

I enter my information into her contacts, then ring my number so I have hers before handing it back. "Text me when you get home so I know you're safe."

"Okay." She clutches at me like she doesn't want to let me go.

But I know what's right, and going home with Ruby isn't it. "If I don't hear from you, I'll call."

"I'll text you." She looks up at me with wide eyes. "I promise."

"Good girl." The words automatic and without thought.

Her eyes grow wide as saucers and she shivers a bit. I put her in the car before I do anything stupid. I buckle her in and her head falls back against the seat. She blinks those big blue eyes at me.

"Ruby?" The moment, the possibility simmers between us, but I don't take it.

"Yes?" Her voice is a husky whisper.

I want to say a thousand things, but only say, "Get home safe, I'll be waiting to hear from you."

"Okay. Good night, Chad."

"Good night." Then I stand back and watch her drive away.

ABOUT THE AUTHOR

Jennifer Dawson grew up in the suburbs of Chicago and graduated from DePaul University with a degree in psychology. She met her husband at the public library while they were studying. To this day she still maintains she was NOT checking him out. Now, over twenty years later they're married, living in a suburb right outside of Chicago with two awesome kids and a crazy dog.

Despite going through a light FM, poem writing phase in high school, Jennifer never grew up wanting to be a writer (she had more practical aspirations of being an international super spy). Then one day, suffering from boredom and disgruntled with a book she'd been reading, she decided to put pen to paper. The rest, as they say, is history.

These days, Jennifer can be found sitting behind her computer writing her next novel, chasing after her kids, keeping an ever watchful eye on her ever growing to-do list, and NOT checking out her husband.